Summer Desires

Emily King

BELLA
BOOKS

2019

Bella Books, Inc.
P.O. Box 10543
Tallahassee, FL 32302

Printed in the United States of America on acid-free paper.

First Bella Books Edition 2019

Editor: Medora MacDougall
Cover Designer: Judith Fellows

ISBN: 978-1-64247-070-3

Other Bella Books by Emily King

Cracking Love

Acknowledgments

A thank you to Bella Books and to my readers. Also, a thank you to Ann Roberts and to Medora MacDougall.

About the Author

Emily King grew up in one of the many farming towns in California's central valley. She attended pharmacy school in southern California and practiced pharmacy for a number of years. She has also worked in farming and now writes fiction. In her spare time, she enjoys cooking with the bounty of food found at the local farmers' market, reading, getting in a good workout, and catering to the whims of her cat.

CHAPTER ONE

As Sarah Wagner bent to collect a discarded bottle cap from the sand of South Coast Beach with her garden-gloved hand, she caught sight of a dark shape partially covered by a tangle of seaweed. With a startled cry, she jumped back, instinctively realizing it was a sea animal of some sort and might be dangerous.

"What is it? What happened?" Justin Morgan called to her as he rushed over.

Sarah pointed at the wide, flat shape in the sand. It wasn't moving, and her fright turned to concern. She set down her Earth Day trash-collecting bucket and walked a little closer. Flies were buzzing in the area but dispersed at her approach.

Justin set down his own bucket and joined her in front of the animal.

They peered down at it. "It's dead, isn't it? Poor thing."

Justin nodded. "Yes, it looks like it's been here a while. It looks like a stingray."

"A stingray?" Sarah repeated. She knew what those were, having seen pictures of them at some point in her life, but she had never seen one in the flesh. Animals with two broad, flat fins that let them almost fly through the water weren't something she had encountered growing up in Iowa.

"Yeah, a stingray," Justin said. "A young one, from the size of it. I wonder what happened to it that it washed up on shore. Maybe a predator got hold of it and injured it." Justin was a southern California and South Coast Beach native and clearly knew something about marine life. Bending down, he carefully reached out with one of his rose-patterned, garden-gloved hands and moved the seaweed aside. The rest of the creature was revealed, including a long thin tail.

"Oh, cool, look at that!" a young male voice said. Sarah and Justin turned to see a trio of high school-aged boys approaching. They held buckets and wore gloves and appeared to be Earth Day participants too.

"It is cool, isn't it?" Justin said. "But it's a stingray, so be careful." He began telling the boys about it, the teacher in him coming out. Like Sarah, he taught at South Coast Beach Middle School, so these high schoolers weren't their students, but it was great to be around kids of any age who were interested in learning. Sarah listened as Justin finished cautioning them about its stinging mechanism and venom, now very glad that she hadn't inadvertently stepped on that part of it.

"Where's its mouth?" one of the boys asked.

"Underneath. Let me get something so I can turn it over, and I'll show you."

Another of the boys picked up a nearby piece of driftwood and handed it to Justin. "Here's a stick."

The shrill sound of a whistle cut through the air. A brunette in red athletic pants and jacket raced toward them, waving her hands as if to tell them to stop what they were doing. She must be one of the SCB lifeguards; she had official-looking emblems on her clothes and was coming from the direction of one of the lifeguard towers that dotted the beach.

"Don't touch that!" the lifeguard's voice carried across the sand. Her arms and legs pumped as she ran toward them. Sarah watched her fit figure approach, rapt. It was too bad the morning was cloudy and brisk; she could just imagine how amazing she would look running in warm weather attire, like shorts and a tight T-shirt or maybe even only a swimsuit. Sarah offered a smile as the lifeguard neared.

She stopped before them, her sunglasses-covered gaze stern. Sarah stopped smiling.

"I'll take that stick, please." She all but grabbed it from Justin.

Justin frowned. "Hey, take it easy. They only wanted to see…"

"So, you were going to poke at it? Don't you know stingrays can be dangerous?"

"Yes, but—"

"Enough said." She ushered everyone back from the stingray and then surveyed the assembled group. "Did anyone get stung or otherwise injured?"

The kids shook their heads and answered, "No."

"Good." She cast an accusatory look at Justin and Sarah. "We want everyone to stay safe. If you see anything else potentially dangerous like this during Earth Day, or any other day for that matter, please just mark the area and alert one of us so we can remove it."

It was clear she was dismissing everyone so that she could take care of her tasks. The kids murmured agreement and wandered away, and Justin moved away too. Sarah started to follow, but hesitated and then stepped forward. "You didn't let him finish what he was saying. Those kids were interested, and he's a teacher."

"Oh? What does he teach?"

Sarah paused. "That doesn't matter."

The lifeguard folded her arms across her tall, strong-looking body and again fixed her with that stern gaze. "So, not biology or anything like that?"

"English," Sarah admitted. She didn't bother mentioning that she was a teacher, too, since she didn't teach something the lifeguard would find relevant either. "But that doesn't mean he doesn't know about stingrays," she quickly added.

The lifeguard shook her head.

"He was going to show them—" Sarah stopped herself from explaining and sighed. The lifeguard wasn't going to listen right now. Some people were just stubborn. Stubborn, but seriously hot. Sarah had the sudden urge to run her hands through her soft-looking, short, sable brown hair, pull her closer, and kiss her. But that was crazy. Sarah didn't get urges like that with complete strangers. She hadn't even felt so strongly about Robin, her last girlfriend.

The lifeguard seemed to be regarding her more closely now, but it was hard to tell with her eyes hidden behind those sunglasses. "Next time, let a lifeguard handle it. I don't want anyone getting hurt on my watch."

"Okay," Sarah said. At least the lifeguard was stubborn for a reason. It was probably stressful keeping an eye on so many beachgoers. Or maybe she was just having a bad day.

Sarah turned and left to catch up with Justin. But she couldn't resist one glance back. Pleasantly surprised to catch the lifeguard's gaze, Sarah tried offering her a smile again. This time, she returned the smile.

Amy Bergen watched the curvaceous blonde catch up to the guy she was with and sighed. No matter how attractive some of the participants were, Earth Day was going to be a long one if they let their curiosity get the best of them while combing the beach for trash. Even though picking up litter seemed straightforward, it wasn't without risk. The volunteers were instructed at the beginning of the day not to touch hazardous items and instead mark the area for professional pickup, but they sometimes couldn't resist and ended up getting injured and requiring first aid or more. There was always someone who found something dangerous, such as that stingray or a used condom or even medical waste like a syringe with an attached needle. She and the other lifeguards regularly removed dangerous objects from the beach, but it was hard to get it all. She felt fortunate to have reached this group in time to avert an incident.

Although she had managed to prevent anyone from getting injured, Amy wished she hadn't spoken so sharply to them; they clearly meant well since they had come to participate in the beach cleanup. It was just that lots of people coming to a hazardous scene only made preventing injury more challenging. She had wanted to break up the group before a larger crowd gathered. And she was worried about what they intended to do with that stick. In her experience, people with sticks usually got up to no good at the beach. She may have slightly misjudged the level of danger in this situation, but as a new lifeguard she wasn't taking any chances.

Having completed the removal of the stingray, she walked back to her tower to watch her area of the beach and ocean for other potential problems. Her assigned zone was clear right now and her thoughts returned to the woman.

What the woman had said about the kids being interested echoed in her mind. She was right; this had been a missed opportunity to teach them. As someone who had participated in the SCB junior lifeguard program as a kid and who had recently applied to become an instructor in the same program, she was going to have to do better than this. She was out of practice that was all. She had spent too much time in the business world ordering people around—and too much time away from the lifeguard program while she toiled in the family business as owner and manager of a luxury auto dealership. She would do better next time out here.

Curious as to where the blonde was now, she picked up her binoculars. She and the guy she was with had been heading toward the pier. Adjusting the binoculars, she took a peek out of her assigned zone to see what they were doing.

After spotting them, she watched for a moment. They walked slowly, scanning the sand, searching for debris. Fortunately, they didn't seem to be finding anything else that was potentially dangerous. Amy let her eyes linger on the attractive woman. Her golden hair was pulled back in a loose ponytail, revealing her pretty face, and her body was exactly the right amount of curvy in all the right places.

Reminding herself that she was here to work, not scope out women, Amy pulled her gaze away and turned her binoculars back to her zone.

After spending the rest of the morning collecting trash, Sarah and Justin took their buckets to the Earth Day garbage drop-off area at the pier.

"Ms. Wagner!" A young voice called.

Sarah turned, searching for the source of the excited cry. She recognized an approaching girl as one of her seventh-graders. "Hi, Hannah!" Sarah smiled at her student, an energetic girl who wore her light brown hair center parted with French-braided pigtails on each side.

"Hi, Ms. Wagner! We're collecting trash, too!" Hannah held up a bucket.

"Hi," said the man accompanying her, a dark-haired and fit-looking guy of about thirty. He gave Sarah an easy smile, setting down his own bucket. "I'm Hannah's uncle, Peter Grandin." He removed his trash-collecting glove and extended his hand.

Sarah removed her glove as well and shook his hand. "Pleased to meet you. I'm Sarah Wagner."

"Hannah tells me you're one of her teachers."

"Yes, she's in my pre-algebra class. She's a good student." Sarah smiled at Hannah, who beamed at the praise.

"That's wonderful." Peter patted Hannah's shoulder.

From the corner of her eye, Sarah noticed Justin practically vibrating at the prospect of meeting Peter. Clearly, he had recovered from the chastising they had received earlier. Since he was part of the reason they'd gotten in trouble, though, Sarah couldn't resist prolonging his wait for an introduction to the hunky guy in front of him by presenting him to Hannah first.

"Hannah, this is my friend, Mr. Morgan, one of the English teachers at our school."

"Hi, Mr. Morgan," Hannah said. "I have Ms. Smith for English."

Justin returned her greeting and shook her hand, smiling. He then looked at Sarah expectantly.

Unable to delay any longer, Sarah introduced him to Peter. "Hello." Peter shook Justin's hand. "So, you teach English?"

"Yes," Justin said, smiling. "Seventh and eighth grade. What do you do?"

"Uncle Peter's a lifeguard!" Hannah interjected.

"Oh, mm-hm," Justin said, sounding very interested and taking the opportunity to sweep his gaze over Peter. "And are you here in your official capacity today?" he asked with a flirtatious tilt of his head.

"No, I'm off today. Just spending the day with Hannah and helping clean up the beach," Peter replied. Sarah had the feeling Justin was wasting his efforts with him, because he wasn't showing anything other than friendly interest. It looked like neither she nor Justin was going to have much luck finding a date today. Not that finding dates was the goal of Earth Day, but Sarah had been open to the idea and she knew Justin had been too.

"Ms. Wagner?" Hannah spoke. "Are you and Mr. Morgan doing the Fun Run next month?"

Sarah glanced at Justin, hoping he would tell her what that was, but he was still busy trying to assess the effect of his charms on Peter. She turned back to Hannah. "What's the Fun Run?"

Peter spoke first. "It's one of the fundraisers for the SCB junior lifeguard program. Hannah's going to try out for the program this year."

"Good for you, Hannah," Sarah said. "I'd be glad to do the Fun Run." An image of the gorgeous, running lifeguard from this morning popped into her mind. Would she be there, too? Sarah would welcome another chance to meet her, especially under the friendlier circumstances of a fundraiser.

"I'd be glad to do the Fun Run, too," Justin said.

"Cool." Hannah grinned at them.

"How far is it?" Sarah asked.

"Five kilometers."

Sarah couldn't hold back a small grimace at realizing the distance was three miles. She was fit to an extent, but it was from riding her bicycle along the local bike paths, not jogging.

"It's on the beach," Hannah added.

"That sounds good," Justin said.

"It will be," Hannah enthused. "It's going to raise a lot of money. Uncle Peter helps run the junior lifeguard program. If I get into it, I get to jump off the pier at the end!"

"Really?" Sarah asked in surprise. The SCB pier was a very tall pier as well as one of the longest on the West Coast.

Peter nodded. "All of the junior lifeguards get to jump off the pier, if they'd like to. But the main goal of the program is to teach kids water safety skills. We instruct kids in a variety of lifeguarding skills, everything from different aquatic skills to rescue skills to first aid. The program involves both teamwork and leadership and a lot of physical conditioning. We're expecting about a thousand students this year."

"Wow," Sarah said. If it was that many students, there were probably a lot of other kids from SCB Middle School participating.

"And do the students graduate to become lifeguards?" Justin asked.

"No, not yet. The program does help prepare them for that, though. Some students do the program for fun, and others do the program to develop and practice lifeguarding skills. If being a lifeguard is something they're interested in, they still have to wait until they're old enough and then go through lifeguard tryouts. But those are much, much harder."

Sarah and Justin nodded.

"Ewww," came a voice over the sound of the ocean.

They turned their heads in the direction of the voice. A woman was staring at something in the sand, her lips curled back in disgust.

"I think I'd better go see what's happening," Peter said. "Come on, Hannah." They hurried off, Peter calling over his shoulder, "It was nice to meet you both."

"Likewise," they called back. Justin turned to Sarah and asked, "Do you want to go see what she found?"

"Seriously? After what happened this morning?"

Justin laughed. "I was only kidding."

"Good," Sarah said, shaking her head. "Want to check out the festivities instead?" She indicated the Earth Day displays, vendors, and activities in the plaza by the pier.

Justin eyed the food booths. "Yeah, I'm hungry. Let's get some lunch."

They got drinks and slices of pizza and found a spot to sit. The sun was peeking from behind the marine layer now, and the warmth felt good after the chilly late April morning. Nearby, under the sun's rays, gleamed a display of luxury hybrid vehicles from Bergen Motors, one of the festival sponsors.

"Nice," Justin said, gazing dreamily at the sleek, new automobiles. "Can you see me in that coupe? Hot guy by my side?"

The coupe was indeed a beautiful car. Unfortunately, Sarah now tended to associate expensive coupes with her ex-girlfriend, Robin, and the cars did not hold as much appeal for her as they used to. Robin, with her designer clothes, expensive cars, and multimillion-dollar home, was a high-powered real estate agent who sold luxury homes in South Coast Beach and the other cities of Orange County to a wealthy clientele. Sarah had become swept up in her world of wealth and luxury, and it had not worked out well. Robin used aspects of Sarah's modest upbringing and lifestyle in the Midwest as fodder for endless jokes and stories to tell her friends. Seduced by the trappings of Robin's wealth, Sarah had found it too easy to overlook—for too long—Robin's belittling behavior and faults and those of her friends. She mustered a smile for Justin's benefit. "No," she replied, teasing him, "but I can see myself in that coupe, hot woman by my side, cruising down Pacific Coast Highway, sunroof open…"

Justin laughed good-naturedly but then stopped as he looked at her more closely. With a thoughtful frown, he glanced from her to the expensive cars and back. "Looking at these cars makes you think of Robin, doesn't it?"

"Yeah," Sarah admitted. Justin was all too familiar with her time with Robin, having been there from the start to hear of the excitement of the new relationship, to lend a sympathetic ear when things were going badly between them, and to comfort her when they broke up.

Sarah had met Robin almost immediately after moving to South Coast Beach two years ago. Exploring her new coastal city by strolling along its boulevards and doing some window shopping, she had stopped in front of a boutique to admire the window display after a lacey, sleeveless cocktail dress in dark pink on one of the mannequins caught her eye. It and the other dresses on display were not the kind of clothing one found in the stores of the small farming community in Iowa in which she was raised. In her hometown, what few clothing stores there were displayed mannequins wearing button-down shirts, jeans, and caps emblazoned with the names of tractor companies. Things like her dad wore every day. To buy a nice dress back home necessitated a drive of a couple hours to a larger city. Still, those were not in league with the dresses in this window. And Sarah's salary as a middle school teacher was not in league with the cost of the dresses.

Just as she had been about to turn away from the window display, a woman carrying two large shopping bags had emerged from the boutique. She paused by Sarah's side, gazing at the dress also.

"That's a pretty dress."

"Mm-hm," Sarah murmured, admiring the sheath silhouette and surplice neckline.

"It would look beautiful on you."

Sarah turned to look at the woman then. Intent brown eyes regarded her from an attractive, tanned, and lined, but minimally so, older face. Her short, neatly coiffed hair was reddish brown and she was nattily dressed in tan linen slacks belted at her waist, a navy-blue linen blouse, and tasseled loafers. Tasteful gold jewelry completed her look.

"Why don't you wear that dress and join me for dinner Friday night?"

Sarah felt her eyebrows raise in surprise. "Excuse me?"

"A date. South Coast Steak at seven o'clock."

Sarah tried to process this. Had this woman, a complete stranger who didn't even know if she was a lesbian, just asked her out? Was this how things worked in her new city? Were all the women here so bold? "You don't even know me," Sarah said.

"Ah, but I'd like to know you."

Sarah regarded her, curiosity piqued. She glanced again at the dress. She could easily imagine herself wearing it in the upscale steakhouse and sitting across from this attractive older woman for a nice dinner. But both the dress and the restaurant were out of her price range. She shook her head. "That's nice of you to invite me to dinner, but I'm afraid I can't…"

"Afford the dress?"

Cheeks reddening with embarrassment, Sarah managed to give a short nod.

"Here." The woman handed her one of her shopping bags. "For you. Size eight."

Reflexively, Sarah reached for the bag being handed to her. "What is this? The dress? How did…"

"The owner of the boutique has an accurate eye for size."

Sarah frowned. "This was a little presumptuous, don't you think?" She indicated the bag.

The woman shrugged, apparently unbothered. "I prefer the term audacious. I haven't gotten where I am in life without taking risks and going after what I want."

"What if I'm not interested?" Sarah managed to ask.

"Then keep the dress anyway. But I hope to see you for our dinner date." She turned and walked away.

The conversation was surreal, but Sarah wasn't ready for it to end. "Just dinner?" she called after her.

The woman turned, a smile of victory appearing on her face. "Just dinner."

"I don't even know your name."

"It's Robin."

"Mine's Sarah."

"'Bye for now, Sarah." Robin opened the door of a Porsche 911 Carrera 4S parked at the curb, got in with her remaining shopping bag, and drove away.

"'Bye," Sarah said faintly. The whole encounter had been so out of the realm of anything she had ever experienced that she knew she would wear the dress and meet her for dinner.

True to her word, Robin had not tried to make the evening into anything more than a dinner date. And the date had been pleasant—pleasant enough to result in other dates that had turned into more than just dinner. And that had been pleasant, too—as good, if not better, than things with her previous girlfriend. But Sarah should have known better than to think that anything worthwhile could have come out of being so casually picked up. Now, at the ripe old age of twenty-seven, she liked to think she was a little wiser and would be better at avoiding women like Robin.

She sighed again, trying to push away thoughts of Robin and instead focus on enjoying her pizza with Justin, listening to the live music being played, and watching a group of people doing yoga on the grassy area of the plaza.

Justin brushed off his hands and got to his feet. "I know what will cheer you up. Let's go to the face-painting booth."

Sarah laughed. "Okay." She popped the last bite of her pizza into her mouth and stood up.

After getting rainbows painted on their cheeks, they collected their bikes from the bicycle valet booth and pedaled to Sarah's house. She lived close enough to the beach that when Justin came over, they often walked the few city blocks to the beach and took a staircase down to the sand. The pier was a little further, though, so today they had biked.

At the rental house that she shared with two roommates, Justin said goodbye and kept pedaling to his apartment further into the city. Sarah would have preferred to live by herself, but having roommates was the only way to afford living in a beach city. She hadn't moved all the way to California from the Midwest not to live near the beach. And if she was going to live near the beach, then she was really going to live *at* the beach, not in the inland portion of a beach city. She felt lucky to live in this house, even if it took a sizeable chunk of her salary and meant having less privacy.

She parked her bike in the garage and then headed around to the small backyard to rinse off the bucket and the garden gloves that she had taken to the beach as part of keeping the trash collection during Earth Day a zero-waste event.

An image of the woman from the beach floated into her mind again. She had returned Sarah's smile as they parted, so maybe like Sarah she would welcome another meeting. Sarah wondered if she had already ruined her chances with her, though, because of the stingray incident. That is, if the lifeguard was even a lesbian.

What if she hadn't ruined her chances? The lifeguard was probably stationed in that tower near where she and Justin had been picking up trash, so it should be easy enough to find her again and find out. Sarah just had to muster the courage to try.

CHAPTER TWO

Amy woke but stayed in bed. If she stayed there, she could avoid going to Sunday brunch at her parents' house and avoid hearing another round of criticism from her family about becoming a lifeguard. She wouldn't have to endure their judgment for taking a break from the family business or endure their guilt trips about covering her auto dealership in her absence.

Unfortunately, if she missed brunch, she would face criticism, judgment, and guilt for that too. That was what had happened last Sunday when she'd had to work. Sighing, she turned back the covers and got up.

She paused to pet her orange tabby, Sandy, who lay curled at the foot of the bed. A bit of drool from her mouth had dampened the bedspread again. She had started drooling only recently and Amy was a little worried. She planned to take her to the veterinarian if it got any worse. After petting Sandy once more, she went to the kitchen to get something to eat before brunch.

Brunch was a meal that really didn't work for her and not just because of family drama during the meal. It was too hard to wait until lunch to have breakfast. She liked to have both breakfast and lunch each day, not skip breakfast, give it a new name and move it to lunch. It was just one less thing she had in common with her parents and her sister. She fixed herself some scrambled eggs, toast, sliced fruit, and coffee and sat down to eat.

As she finished eating, she heard the *thunk* of the thick Sunday paper being deposited outside her front door. She put on a robe over her bed clothes and stepped out to get it. An article about the Earth Day cleanup was on the front page. An image of the blonde swaying her hips as she walked along the sand popped into her mind. She had been with a guy, but the two of them had seemed more like friends than a couple. Could she be a lesbian? And would she be at the beach again soon, or had she just been there for the Earth Day event?

Refilling her coffee mug, she took it and the paper out to the table and chairs on her balcony. She took a moment to savor the view of the water and to breathe in the fresh ocean air. She loved her beachfront condo. She had bought a place in South Coast Beach instead of inland near her dealership in Santa Ana even though it had meant a commute of about an hour each way. Living at the beach was worth it. And now, with her change of jobs, she had zero commute; she could walk to work.

Amy saw any number of pretty women at the beach on a given day, so she wasn't sure why her thoughts were lingering on the curvaceous blonde specifically. Maybe it was that she had stood up for her friend and for those kids. And maybe it was that she had just seemed so intent and focused on her trash collecting. Amy wanted to date someone serious and caring like that at this point in her life.

Just before the appointed time for brunch, Amy pulled into the driveway of the three-car garage at her parents' two-story Craftsman-style home. Her parents lived on the other side of

South Coast Beach, where plots of land were larger than those at the beach. She parked her Lexus SUV next to her sister's newer one. While she still had the same SUV that her parents had given her as a college graduation gift, Aurora had long since traded hers in. She liked to get a new model every couple of years. Amy took good care of her older vehicle and thought the recent wax and polish job she had personally given it made it look almost as good as Aurora's new model.

She got out and smoothed her slacks and blouse, her usual attire for Sunday brunch. Starting up the walkway, she readied herself to hear the inevitable criticism about her new job. She wondered if today would also be another day when her family would interrogate her about her love life, or lack thereof and ask when she was ever going to get another girlfriend. Such conversations weren't pleasant, but at least her family was tolerant of her sexuality and had been ever since she had come out during college.

Amy let herself in the front door with her key and walked in. Conversation drifted from the living room, about the auto business as usual. Her parents, sister, and brother-in-law were sitting and chatting with, what looked this week to be, mimosas in hand. "Hi, everyone," she said with a smile.

"Amy! Glad you could make it this Sunday!" her mother exclaimed by way of greeting.

Amy blinked. She hadn't expected the criticism to start so quickly. "Mom, you know I was working last weekend."

Her father spoke. "A definite drawback to not being your own boss in that job like you are at your dealership." He returned to a sales numbers conversation he was having with her sister. Amy sighed and took a seat.

Although her parents were in their sixties, they had no plans to retire any time soon. Her father, Robert, continued to run his original dealership in South Coast Beach. A tall man with an easy smile, he had a full head of hair with only some of it graying. Her mother, Beatrice, ran the second dealership in Newport Beach. Visits to the salon kept her hair a dark brown in a stylish cut that fell past her shoulders and featured long bangs parted to the side, all of which slowed any appearance of aging.

"And how many units did you move this week?" her father asked Aurora, inquiring about the number of vehicles her dealership had sold.

With studied nonchalance, Aurora swept a lock of her salon-highlighted blond hair behind one ear and named a high number.

Their father let out a low whistle. "Impressive!"

Aurora grinned, as she rightfully should. Amy offered her congratulations, as well.

"Thanks," Aurora answered. "And don't worry—we sold plenty at your dealership, too." She liked to remind Amy that they were all working more as they covered running her dealership while she took time off from it to work as a lifeguard. But Amy hadn't asked Aurora or any of them to do so, having planned instead for members of her management team to cover her absence. It was her father who had insisted that family members do the job.

"Now, Aurora…" their mother warned.

"I wasn't worried," Amy said, trying not to let Aurora get under her skin. She already knew that her family had moved plenty of vehicles at her dealership. Just because she was spending time away from her dealership didn't mean she wasn't checking on things. But she really hadn't been worried. Her parents and sister were all very good at sales. She was too. The only difference was that running an auto dealership seemed to come naturally to them, filling each of them with energy and enthusiasm, whereas it only drained her.

"Good." Her mother reached over and patted her knee before rejoining the numbers discussion. Amy looked over at Aurora again and couldn't help but feel a twinge of envy. Aurora, ten years her senior, had long since paid off her own loan for her dealership. For Amy, on just a lifeguard salary now, paying off her loan was going to be impossible to do quickly enough to meet the terms of the loan. While being an open water lifeguard paid fairly well, especially as one acquired more skills and certifications and moved up the career ladder, it did not pay nearly as well as being the owner and general manager of a successful luxury auto dealership.

To pay off her loan, she was either going to have to find a buyer for her dealership, which would not only incur the ire of her rather controlling family but also would take some time, or she was going to have to eventually resume her role as general manager and earn that salary in addition to her ownership income. And she was going to have to figure it all out soon in order to continue being a lifeguard, something she very much wanted to do.

"Brunch is ready," Emilia Alvarez, her parents' housekeeper, announced from the doorway. Her apron was immaculate and her hair was pulled back in a tidy bun as always. Emilia had worked in a hotel kitchen at one point and knew much about preparing brunch. She had come to work for Amy's parents because she wanted to slow down and have lighter duties. Amy thought her parents were lucky to have a kind and reliable person like Emilia in their employ.

They made their way to the dining room. Her father took a seat at the head of the table and her mother a seat at the opposite end. Aurora sat to their father's right, her husband Fred at her side. He was a manager at a telecom company in Irvine, the city where Aurora's dealership was located. Amy took her seat to her father's left, an empty chair by her side. She supposed things could be worse—her parents could be trying to fill the chair by setting her up on blind dates.

"Thank you, Emilia," Amy said as she served them each a beautiful plate of blanched asparagus topped with ribbons of prosciutto artfully arranged to nestle a poached egg, all of which was drizzled with hollandaise sauce. Toast points were arrayed along the edge of each plate. Emilia came around with a pitcher to refill the glasses of mimosas but brought Amy a flute of plain orange juice, knowing that she preferred it to the cocktail. Consuming too much alcohol didn't mesh with Amy's fitness regimen, so she drank only occasionally. Once everyone was served, her father raised his glass and made one of his usual toasts about another successful week in the auto business.

With one of the trimmed pieces of toast, Amy dabbed up some of the hollandaise and popped it in her mouth. The food was delicious, as always. It alone was reason enough to come to brunch. She'd already had toast and eggs for breakfast, but Emilia took them to another level.

"You're awfully quiet over there, Amy," Aurora said.

Amy raised her head to find her sister's gaze and everyone else's gazes on her. Having been lost in her thoughts while enjoying her food, she had no idea what the topic of conversation was. In truth, she hadn't been making the effort to pay attention. She didn't feel like she was part of many of the conversations at brunch anymore now that she had taken a different job.

At previous brunches, she had tried telling some work stories and describing her activities as a lifeguard, but her family's only responses had been some polite nods and a few utterances of "Is that so?" so she had stopped mentioning any of it—including the very important fact that she had changed over from her initial seasonal lifeguard position to a permanent one. She knew they wouldn't take that news well at all.

But she was happier at work than she had been in quite a while; she wished she hadn't waited so long to explore her childhood dream of becoming a lifeguard. She was only thirty-one: not at all too old to start a new career path. She hoped to take this new career path even further by becoming an instructor in the junior lifeguard program.

The SCB junior lifeguard program was what had enamored Amy of lifeguarding. Starting in junior high school, she had done the program each summer. Initially, her parents had been wary of signing her up for the program because they wanted her to work in the family business, not grow up to become a lifeguard. But she had reassured them that she just wanted to swim, kayak, surf, and do all of the other things that kids got to do in the program, not become a lifeguard, and they had relented. They couldn't very well argue against practicing swimming and other water skills.

It wasn't until subsequent years, as Amy excelled in the program and eventually reached junior lifeguard captain status with Peter, her best friend then and still, that the thought of becoming a lifeguard seriously entered her mind. However, she had been thrown for a loop when Peter professed his love for her their final year of the program. She and Peter had been close, but she had no idea that he felt the way he did. She hadn't thought of him romantically and it was hard to tell him that without hurting him. What she wanted to say but didn't feel that she could at that point in her life in high school was that she wasn't into *any* guy romantically, despite having dated a few. She already knew that she preferred females. The whole ordeal made their senior year very awkward and going off to college to get away held a lot of appeal. The decision to do so was made even easier when her performance on the high school swim team netted her a scholarship. She made the decision to major in business administration, because her family business was what she knew. Peter stayed in South Coast Beach and became a lifeguard.

She and Peter lost touch that first year she was away at college, but as soon as she came back for summer break, they ran into each other at the beach. The encounter was strained, but when she gathered her courage and came out to him, he gave her a big hug and things had been immediately better between them. They stayed in touch over her remaining college years and when Peter fell in love with another woman, Amy was very happy for him. She attended his wedding and met his wife, Tammy, a manager of a department store. Amy's and Peter's renewed closeness fortunately didn't seem to bother Tammy.

Seeing Peter's happiness as a lifeguard as she worked, not so happily, at her dealership had made Amy wonder what it would have been like had she also stayed and become a lifeguard. She said as much to Peter one day and he encouraged her to find out. At first, she laughed. She knew what lifeguard tryouts consisted of: things like timed 1,000-yard and 500-yard open water swims and a 1,500-yard continuous run-swim-run. The 500-yard swim would be similar to the 500-meter freestyle that she used to swim in both high school and college, but the 1,000-yard swim would be another matter. One thousand yards was just over 900 meters, which was eighteen laps of an Olympic-size pool. While she still swam and maintained a certain level of fitness with windsurfing and other activities, her college swim team days were behind her. She would have a lot of training to do to be competitive against what she knew would be a few hundred other very good swimmers vying for the available lifeguard positions, especially since swimming in the cold, choppy ocean was a lot different than swimming in a pool.

The thought of doing the lifeguard tryouts stayed in her mind, though. She soon created a training regimen for herself. Countless beach runs, sprints, swims, pushups, lunges, and planks later, she got herself into competitive shape again. It felt good. She joined Peter in some of his workouts, and by the time lifeguard tryouts arrived in January she was ready. The ocean temperature on the day of tryouts was a bracing fifty-eight degrees Fahrenheit, but the most difficult thing about the timed open ocean swims was swimming in such close quarters with the frenzied crowd of contenders. There were no marked lanes in the ocean like there were in a swimming pool. It was a free-for-all of rapidly churning arms and legs, and she was accidentally kicked in the face a couple of times. Despite the difficulties, she placed well enough in the tryouts to be able to interview that very day. When she was hired, it felt like she finally had a job that fit.

She supposed she could try telling her family about her renewed interest in the junior lifeguard program. "So…I submitted an application to become an instructor for the junior lifeguard program."

Her father looked up from his meal and squinted at her. "That thing you did when you were a kid?"

"Yes, but this time I would be one of the instructors."

"Huh."

She wished she hadn't said anything. She didn't know if her dad or the rest of her family would ever understand that she had dreams and passions outside the family business. And she was already nervous about her application for the junior lifeguard instructor position. It was a bit of a long shot this early on. She only had three months under her belt as a lifeguard after receiving her general lifeguard training, which was the bare minimum amount of time required to be eligible as an instructor for the junior lifeguard program, but she hoped that with what she felt was a strong performance in the interview, her history with the program, her good job standing, and a recommendation from Peter, who was the assistant coordinator for the program, she would get one of the few positions open this spring. It would be very satisfying to give back to the program that had given her so much during childhood, and she was eagerly awaiting the day when the hiring decisions would be announced.

Amy wracked her brain for a safer topic of conversation, one that would interest her single-minded family. Remembering the crowd that she had seen admiring the display of luxury vehicles from her dealership at the plaza by the pier yesterday, she spoke again. "I wonder how much extra foot traffic and sales the dealership will see from my display of hybrids at the Earth Day event yesterday."

"Oh, so you're already missing the business?" Aurora asked.

Amy took a breath. She should have known her comment would draw a jab even though she had signed on as a sponsor for the SCB Earth Day event almost a year in advance, long before she had taken her lifeguard job. She had asked her parents and sister if they wanted to participate and bring vehicles from their dealerships as well, but they had declined, saying it would be a waste of time and money. She didn't understand their resistance; people who were interested enough to participate in Earth Day would be exactly the type of people who would be interested enough in green technology to buy a hybrid vehicle.

She had ignored her family's protestations and decided to sponsor the event herself, having grown more and more tired of everyone trying to tell her how to run her business. She liked having the ability to support the community event while at the same time being able to enhance awareness of her dealership and potentially attract new customers. Her family was more comfortable with more traditional marketing ideas. It was just as well; they had yet to fully embrace green technology, so none of their dealerships carried the full line of hybrids anyway.

Amy decided to ignore her sister's jab. "The sales guy I had working the event said he thought the display went over very well. A handful of people even made appointments to come in for test drives."

Her father cleared his throat. "If there's an increase in sales, it certainly won't be enough to pay off your dealership loan."

Amy took another breath. "Of course not, Dad," she replied in a more reasonable tone than the comment warranted. Her father constantly reminded her that she owed money to the bank. He had co-signed the loan to finance the startup of her dealership, just as he had years ago for Aurora. Apparently, he now thought Amy would default and stick him with the remainder of the loan payments. She wished he knew that she would never let things come to that point.

"Don't worry, I'll pay off the loan, just like I paid off the one for my condo." Amy was very glad that the condo was hers free and clear. She wished that she were there right now, instead of at this table facing the ongoing disapproval of her family. At her condo, the only disapproval she encountered was when she tried to give Sandy a flavor of cat food other than chicken. She wondered if she could use the excuse of needing to go shopping for a new blanket for Sandy in order to leave brunch early.

CHAPTER THREE

Sarah sat at a table in the teachers' lounge before the start of the school day, sipping coffee from her commuter mug and chatting with the other teachers.

"Happy Monday, everyone," Justin said as he breezed through the door. The other teachers, many of whom had not yet had their quota of coffee, responded with mostly grunted greetings. He took a seat by Sarah.

"And happy Monday to you," Sarah said. "You're more chipper than usual this morning. What's up?"

"Must be my invigorating bike ride to work."

"You rode your bike?'

"Mm-hm. I'm still feeling inspired by my ride to your house on Earth Day."

Guessing that probably wasn't the whole reason, she waited for more.

"Not only that, but I have to get in shape for that Fun Run next month. I haven't been doing my cardio," he said, making a sad face.

"I better start getting ready for that, too. I went online and registered for the run, but I haven't done much jogging yet."

"I registered, too. Want to go for a jog this coming weekend?"

"Sure, how about on Sunday?"

"A Sunday jog." Justin tapped his chin thoughtfully. "I'll have to cancel my Sunday drive, but I like it. I'll ride my bike over again."

Marsha Jackson, one of the physical education teachers, came to stand near them at the table. "You're doing the Fun Run, did you say?"

"Yes," Sarah answered. "It's to raise money for the city's junior lifeguard program."

Marsha nodded. "I know. I'm doing it, too. I wondered if you would like flyers for the program to post in your classrooms. I've already posted them around the locker rooms and have some extras."

"Can we do that?" The school had policies about posting things for which entrance fees were involved.

"Oh, yes, it's fine. I post them every year. The program has a certain number of scholarships for kids whose families can't pay the registration fee. That's part of what the Fun Run raises money for, you know."

"Oh, okay," Sarah said. "I'm still learning about the program. I'd be glad to put up a flyer."

"Me, too," Justin said.

"Great, I'll give them to you at lunch break."

After lunch, Sarah returned to her classroom with the promised flyer. She began taping it to a prominent space on the wall as her eighth-grade algebra students started filing in. She turned to greet them and then returned to her task. When finished, she took a seat at her desk and began leafing through her lesson plan, idly listening as students commented on the flyer. Many sounded interested.

After she took roll call, one of her students raised her hand.

"Yes, Mandy?" Sarah said. Mandy was also originally from the Midwest and had moved here even more recently than

Sarah. She was a good student, but Sarah worried that she was having trouble fitting in.

"Ms. Wagner, I saw the lifeguard poster and I was just wondering...do lifeguards use algebra?"

Sarah blinked. That was not a question that she had anticipated getting as a result of posting the flyer, even from Mandy. However, this was a math class, so it wasn't unreasonable for the students to wonder how the junior lifeguard program pertained. There were a few titters from Mandy's classmates, but Sarah knew that she was asking out of curiosity rather than to be difficult. She hastened to answer before Mandy became embarrassed. "In the normal course of their jobs, no, I wouldn't think that lifeguards use algebra. Basic math skills are probably enough."

"Oh," Mandy said, sounding disappointed.

"However," Sarah said, approaching the dry erase board and picking up one of the markers there, "advanced math skills like we're learning can be useful in almost any situation—even at the beach." She didn't want to pass up the opportunity to maintain Mandy's apparent interest in the tryouts, because it seemed like tryouts and the junior lifeguard program could be a great place for Mandy or even the other students to make more friends from the area.

Uncapping the marker, she wrote out a math problem involving how long it would take a lifeguard—she had in mind a very specific, very gorgeous lifeguard on South Coast Beach—to get to a rescue by a certain route that involved a combination of running and swimming. After taking her students through the problem and answering questions, she hoped she had piqued their interest further. She made a mental note to try and follow up with the lifeguard from the beach to make sure she had provided correct information to her students about lifeguards and math.

CHAPTER FOUR

Amy walked up the ramp of her lifeguard tower Sunday morning, glad to be at work and not brunch this week. She hung her rescue can, her main piece of lifeguard equipment, on the hook on the tower's eave. The "can," a red plastic float with handles, was attached to a line and harness and could be used during rescue as a flotation device or for signaling. She unlatched and opened the window coverings on the front and sides of the tower's cabin, unlocked the tower door, and let herself in.

Cool air greeted her and Amy gave a brief shiver. Like the beach itself, the tower was often chilly in the morning. Amy envied Sandy her new blanket, snuggly and warm. After she had washed and dried it so as not to offend Sandy with new blanket smells, she had arranged it on the bed. Sandy had sniffed it suspiciously but laid down on it. As soon as she had felt the soft, fuzzy material, she had rolled around on it in delight and started kneading it with her front paws. Seeing that had put a big smile on Amy's face and made her glad she had bought another exactly like it for Sandy's favorite spot on the couch. Sandy was enjoying the little blanket so much that Amy was tempted to get one for herself.

Settling into her chair at her tower windows, Amy started scanning her assigned area. This early in the day, mostly walkers and joggers populated the beach. Occasionally, someone ventured out ankle deep to feel the water, but the only people swimming now were a few body boarders wearing wetsuits. The surfers were down by the pier, out of her zone. Some seagulls took flight with a squawk when a man searching for trinkets and treasures with a metal detector got too close. The birds glided on the breeze before resettling themselves further away. Later, when the sun came through the marine layer around lunch time, Amy knew that sunbathers, families, and more beachgoers would arrive.

Sarah rummaged through her dresser drawer, trying to find the one pair of jogging shorts she knew was in there somewhere. When her hand grasped a piece of slippery fabric, she pulled. Examining her find, she realized it was a negligee that Robin had given her. Sarah thought that she had gotten rid of everything from Robin, but apparently, she had missed a piece.

Her roommates, Fiona Peng and Susie Truong, would be alarmed by this forgotten piece of a past bad relationship. Both were big believers in feng shui and some of their belief had rubbed off on Sarah. Feng shui, Sarah had learned, was the art of object placement to support the flow of energy. Old, unwanted lingerie lurking in a dresser drawer meant that stagnant energy was present.

Thank goodness Fiona and Susie were at work this weekend, as they were most weekends, in the hospital where they worked as pharmacy interns, and not here to see this problem, small as it may be. Not that Sarah was in the habit of showing them her lingerie, but still.

Fiona, in particular, had emphasized to Sarah the importance of getting rid of any remnants of her time with her ex so as to not block opportunities for a new relationship with someone else. Sarah set the negligee aside to donate to the thrift store at her next opportunity. She wasn't sure if this lingering evidence of her relationship with Robin had been having ill effects on her love life, but it couldn't be helping.

She resumed digging in the drawer, emitting a triumphant cry when she finally found her jogging shorts. She held them up for inspection—and remembered why she rarely wore them: they were very short shorts. They were a pretty shade of blue, though, with turquoise piping, and there was a matching turquoise top. After getting dressed in them, she pulled on socks and her running shoes and went outside to get warmed up with some exercises. Justin was riding his bike over and would already be warmed up when he arrived.

Justin rolled up Sarah's driveway on his bike with a broad smile and then hopped off and scanned her outfit. "Oooh, decided to show some leg today, huh?" he asked by way of greeting.

"Well…" Sarah shuffled around self-consciously.

"No, no, you look hot in those shorts. You'll have the women at the beach drooling. I wanted to wear my short shorts too today for the guys, but they weren't a length suitable for biking, if you know what I mean."

Sarah laughed. "Well, you made the right decision. We can't have you arrested for indecent exposure when we have all of this training to do."

"Definitely not," he said with a shake of his head.

"Let's put your bike in the garage, and we'll go."

They started their run at a slow pace, using the few city blocks to the beach to get their jogging legs. "Which way do you want to go?" he asked when they stopped at a traffic signal.

"If the Fun Run is going to be on the beach, maybe we should do some jogging on the sand," Sarah said. Besides, she wanted to talk to that hot lifeguard.

"Want to jog down to the pier and get onto the beach there?"

"Okay, let's do that." Sarah tried a faster pace now that they were warmed up. It was tough to maintain all the way to the pier, but she wanted this training to be productive. Arriving at the pier, she stopped, breathing hard.

"Whew," Justin panted, stopping alongside her. "Maybe I shouldn't have ridden my bike over. I think I'm worn out already."

She worked at catching her breath, too. "Yeah, I thought I was in decent shape from cycling, but I think jogging is a different animal."

"Dodging all the people on the sidewalk wasn't making it easy."

"Maybe running on the beach will be better."

"Yeah, let's try it."

They took the stairs down to the beach, making their way through the loose sand to the more compact sand of the shoreline, where they resumed their run.

Amy scanned her zone from within her lifeguard tower, her gaze stopping on a boy stumbling through the sand. He looked to be about three or four years old and was clearly intent on making his way to the water. She searched the area around him, looking for an adult who might be accompanying him. Not seeing one, she grabbed her red rescue can from its hanger, hastened down the tower's ramp, and jogged in his direction.

When the boy reached firmer sand at the shoreline and got his footing, he immediately ran after a receding wave, heedless of the incoming ones. Amy sprinted to the boy and snatched him up in her free arm just as a wave came rolling in.

"Whoa there, little guy." She turned her body to shield them both from the oncoming wave. The wave was thigh-high on her but was head-high on him. It would have easily knocked him off his feet and pulled him under. The crashing wave jolted her a bit, but she maintained her footing. The boy started crying, no doubt at the surprise of being snatched up and then at the jarring from the wave.

"It's okay. I've got you." Amy carried him up to shore against the pull of the receding surf. Upon reaching dry sand, she set him down and knelt beside him, keeping hold of him while she looked him over to make sure he was all right. "Are you hurt?" she asked, suspecting he was crying only from surprise and fear, not injury.

"No," he sniffled.

"Good," she said. "My name's Amy. What's yours?"

"Bobby." He sniffled again.

"Bobby, it's not safe for you to run out into the water alone. Are you here with someone today, maybe your mommy or daddy?"

"Daddy. Daddy's sleeping."

Amy assumed that meant his father was dozing somewhere nearby on the crowded beach on a towel or in a chair in the afternoon sun. "Do you—"

"Bobby! There you are!" A sunburned middle-aged man said as he hurried over to Bobby. He looked at Amy. "Did something happen?"

Amy stood and explained what had transpired and he thanked her for her help. She advised him not to leave his child unattended near the water, even if lifeguards were present. It was obvious from his compressed lips and crossed arms that he didn't like being told this, but he needed to hear it. She watched him walk away with Bobby, then turned and walked back to the tower.

As Sarah and Justin jogged, Sarah kept an eye on the towers they passed, trying to see which one belonged to the lifeguard she wanted to talk to. The towers looked a lot alike, so it was difficult to tell exactly which one they had been near on Earth Day, but she thought it might be the one coming up. With the beach so crowded today, though, it was hard to know for sure.

Her legs burning from running on the sand, which was even harder than running on pavement, Sarah slowed her stride. "Let's take a break," she said, breathing hard.

"You read my mind," Justin said, breathing just as hard and slowing to a walk beside her.

"Why don't we go up to the dry sand and sit down for a moment or two?" She led him up away from the shoreline.

Winding their way through the other beachgoers, they found a slightly less crowded area not far from the tower she thought was the right one.

Justin plopped himself onto the sand, and Sarah sat down next to him. "It's a good thing the Fun Run isn't really a race."

"Yeah, we'd be toast."

They sat quietly as they caught their breath. "You know," Justin said, "I didn't know so many of my students were going to try out for the junior lifeguard program. That flyer I put up in my classroom was a real conversation starter in all of my classes."

"I had the same experience in mine. I've got at least six students that I know of besides Hannah who are doing the tryouts."

"Good, then you won't mind going with me." Justin smiled at her.

"To the tryouts?" she asked.

"Yeah. I might have let slip in class the fact that I live near the high school where the tryouts are being held. That made the students ask if I would help cheer them on. They were so excited that I agreed to stop by and watch."

"That was nice of you."

"So, you'll go with me this Saturday?"

"Sure, why not? We can cheer on all of our students."

They rested quietly for a while longer. No one was outside on the small deck of the lifeguard tower, so if the brunette was the one staffing this tower, she was either inside behind the tinted windows or out on the beach. Sarah couldn't very well go up the ramp and try to peer in the windows. That would just make the lifeguard mad again, and she certainly didn't want to do that. What she wanted to do was get an answer to the question her student had about lifeguards and math. Well that, and hopefully summon the courage to flirt a little and possibly ask her out.

Her attention was drawn to someone emerging from a crowd by the shoreline. The woman, who was carrying a small, red, buoy-like object in her hand, wore a red one-piece racing-style swimsuit that revealed a sleek, athletic physique. Without a doubt, it was the lifeguard from Earth Day. Sarah stared, transfixed by the curves and lines of her very fit and attractive body. She continued to watch as the woman's toned thighs and calves took her up the ramp of the lifeguard tower, admiring the definition in her arm and shoulder as she reached one arm up to hang the buoy on the eaves of the tower.

Justin was watching now, too. "Hey, isn't that the lifeguard from Earth Day?" He had mostly forgiven the lifeguard for snapping at him during the stingray find. Sarah had recounted some of her conversation with her to him, explaining that she had seemed a little stressed out and simply hadn't wanted anyone to get hurt.

Sarah nodded and felt herself blush.

Justin tilted his head and regarded her with interest, a smile growing on his face. "Oh, you wanted to see her again."

"Maybe." She smiled back.

"You know," he said in a chatty tone, "now that it's May, there's only one more month before classes let out for summer. I think now could be as good a time as any if someone wanted to—I don't know—do something like start a summer fling with a lifeguard."

Sarah turned to face him. "You know flings aren't my thing—even if that lifeguard is seriously hot." She watched as she opened the tower door and went inside.

"I know, I know. You want a nice relationship." He shook his head.

"Is that so bad?" Sarah asked. Her attention was drawn to the tower again as the woman emerged with a chair, placed it in a sunny area on the deck, and took a seat.

"No, but I'll tell you from experience that a summer fling can be refreshing." He bumped her shoulder playfully. "Like a nice rosé wine," he added in a flippant tone.

"What? Like a nice rosé?" Sarah let out a laugh and visualized the pink wine. "Do tell—how so?"

"Oh, you know," he said with studied casualness. "Pretty to look at, a little something light and friendly to stimulate the senses, nothing too serious."

Sarah laughed again, hoping that he was mostly kidding. "Oh, boy, that's quite a comparison. With wine talk like that, next you'll be telling me about flavors and mouth feel."

"You mean you don't want to hear about subtle—"

She elbowed him to cut off his words.

He laughed. "Okay, okay."

Near the tower, a group of guys started what looked like an impromptu game of soccer in the sand. "Mmm, some eye candy for me, too," he said.

With idle interest, Sarah watched the guys kick the soccer ball around. The guys glanced frequently toward the lifeguard tower, as did Sarah. It became obvious that they were mostly playing to impress, with each of them trying to judge the effects his moves might be having on the female in the chair on the deck. She turned to Justin. "Don't get too excited about your eye candy. I think every one of them is straight."

"Even the one in the pink shorts?"

"Definitely straight. He's only playing for the lifeguard. Watch."

Pink Shorts intercepted the ball. He made a show of bouncing the ball from knee to knee, then bounced it to the top of his head to balance it there for a second, and then let it fall so he could kick it mid-drop. He grinned in the direction of the lifeguard tower. The lifeguard was looking in a different direction, and Pink Shorts' shoulders slumped as he realized that she hadn't watched his display.

"Ugh, you're right," Justin said. "Unfortunately for them, she doesn't seem the least bit interested."

"No," Sarah agreed. She watched the others vie for attention, but the lifeguard scarcely gave them a glance.

"So, there you have it: she's gay," Justin said.

Sarah frowned. "Just because she's not into a bunch of guys playing soccer in front of her tower doesn't mean she's gay." She tried not to sound too irritated at her friend.

"Okay, sorry, maybe that was sexist," Justin admitted. "They do seem a little desperate. I wouldn't be into that, either."

"Yeah," she said. "And she is at work."

"There is also that."

"Speaking of which," she said as she got up from the sand, "I wonder if she can tell me something."

"Tell you something? Tell you what?"

"Just wait here. I'll be right back," she said.

Amy was tired of the soccer players who were doing more posturing than soccer playing in front of her tower. People who viewed her as nothing more than a sex object because she was in a swimsuit at the beach was one of the few things that irked her about the job, almost as much as people who left toddlers unattended to wander into the ocean. As soon as her swimsuit dried from her partial dip in the ocean, she planned to go back inside the tower, hoping that doing so would encourage the group to move to another location.

The guys paused their play and turned to look at something. Amy followed their collective gaze and immediately saw what had drawn their attention: a blond woman in running attire. A very pretty blond woman in very little running attire. One who looked a lot like the woman from the Earth Day cleanup.

So...she had come to the beach again as Amy had hoped. Amy let her gaze linger on her as she walked through the sand, thankful that the sunglasses she had put on before coming out to the deck allowed her to be discreet in her admiration of the woman's lustrous golden hair, lovely face, and luscious body—which was as deliciously curvy as she remembered it to be.

"Hi," one of the guys called to the woman.

"Hi," she called back.

The group had to be happy that their peacocking had finally succeeded in attracting some female attention.

"Did you want to watch us play?" the guy in pink shorts asked.

"No thanks. I just have a question for the lifeguard."

Amy sat up in surprise. The woman was here for her, not them? It wasn't unusual to get questions from the public, but she had thought the woman had been drawn by the guys' little exhibition. Apparently not. Maybe the woman recognized her from Earth Day and had a question about the stingray? Then again, maybe it had nothing to do with Earth Day and she had a question along the usual lines of where it was best to swim or if there were sharks in the water.

The blonde stopped before the front railing of the tower and looked up at her.

"Hi. I remember you," Amy said with a smile as she stood up and walked over. "Can I help you?" She rested her elbows on the railing and looked down at Sarah, thankful again that her roaming gaze was hidden behind sunglasses.

"Hi," the woman answered.

Amy waited for her to say more, but she was just kind of staring at her. As she continued to wait, she felt her smile slipping. From their conversation on Earth Day, she had thought the woman was an intelligent person, but maybe she was as much of an airhead as some of the soccer players seemed to be.

"Um," the woman finally said, "...do lifeguards need to know math?"

Amy straightened. What kind of question was that? Was it some kind of lifeguard joke? She eyed the woman, trying to decide how to answer.

"Uh, I mean algebra?"

Amy frowned. She couldn't imagine what the woman was playing at with her strange question, but she hadn't missed the woman's perusal of her cleavage moments ago. Maybe she was a lesbian like herself. If so, that was nice, but unfortunately it seemed she was just another person who thought it would be cute to flirt with a lifeguard. She had already put up with more than her share of that today from the guys. At least they weren't asking her questions about math, of all things. "Miss, if you don't need assistance, I'm working here." Amy pointedly looked away to resume scanning her zone.

"Well, I'm working too," the woman said in an affronted tone.

What? Amy looked down at her again. She was glaring at her with her hands on her hips. Okay, maybe she wasn't making lifeguard jokes and maybe she wasn't flirting. But then what did she want?

"I'm a math teacher," the woman said, offering a coherent explanation, thankfully. "Some of my students plan to do the junior lifeguard program this summer, and the question of whether lifeguards happen to use algebra came up in class."

"Oh," Amy said, blinking in surprise behind her sunglasses.

"I thought that as long as I was at the beach, I would come by and ask you, but I can see that it was a bad idea." She turned to go.

"No, wait," Amy said, chagrined by her assumptions that the teacher was there to play games. "I misunderstood. I'm sorry."

The woman hesitated, slowly turning back around.

Amy was relieved. "Let me answer your question. Please."

The woman waited.

Amy rested her arms on the railing once more as she contemplated the woman's question. She had had training in higher math and statistics during her business degree coursework, but she knew that wasn't what the woman wanted to know, so she didn't mention it.

"The amount of math we use depends on our duties, but most of it is going to be basic math. The lifeguards who use the most math would be the ones who are paramedics, because they have to figure doses of emergency medications. But algebra isn't used that I know of."

The teacher gave a little nod of her head, seemingly satisfied. "Okay, that's all I needed to know. Thanks."

Amy nodded back with a smile. "You're welcome. And again, I'm sorry about before."

"No problem." She gave a little wave before walking off. Amy didn't know whether it was a wave of dismissal or a wave goodbye or both, but she knew she deserved any indifference the woman might have shown her.

Sarah tromped back to where she had left Justin waiting, still irritated by the initial brush-off she had received from the lifeguard. She didn't know why it had been so hard to get her to answer a simple question. Granted, she had taken long enough to ask it. But her breath had caught and she had become tongue-tied at seeing the lifeguard up close and clad only in a swimsuit this time. The smooth, tanned, golden skin of her toned body... the short, soft-looking, sable brown hair...the pretty planes and curves of her sunglasses-shielded face...and the way her swimsuit brought out her cleavage as she leaned on the railing of her tower... It had all made Sarah's clearly formulated question disappear from her brain and she'd ended up blurting something else instead. Her eventual question had been clear enough, though, and the lifeguard seeming to misunderstand it seemed like just an excuse for not taking Sarah seriously, like so many others had done.

As a woman in the field of math, and not just any woman, but a blond one, she often encountered sexism. If she had a dollar for every blonde joke she had heard from people over the years, she wouldn't have to live with two roommates to pay the rent. It was always more disappointing to encounter it from another woman, though. At least when the lifeguard had finally answered, it had been an answer that she could take back to her students.

Justin stood up at her approach. "Well? What was that all about? Was she able to tell you what you wanted to know?"

"Yes, but it wasn't easy," Sarah said. "And I think you were right, after all—I think she is gay." The lifeguard had been wearing sunglasses, but she had felt her gaze travel over her body, almost like a physical caress, as she had approached the tower. She had felt it again as she'd leaned on the railing to say hello to her. It had felt incredibly tantalizing. She wondered why the warmth had stopped so abruptly when she'd asked her simple question.

"If she's gay, that's good, right?" Justin asked.

"It would be if she weren't also so unfriendly. Come on, let's finish our jog."

* * *

After dinner, as Amy sat in a comfy chair in her condo, trying to read a fitness magazine while Sandy was curled up on her lap, she found herself instead thinking of her interaction with the jogger at the beach. The woman had been on her mind throughout the day, and Amy still felt bad about misreading her.

She wished that she hadn't been so quick to judge the blonde and lump her in with all of the attention-seekers at the beach. Just because there'd been a few instances of flirtatious beachgoers didn't mean that everyone was there to hit on the lifeguards. The fact that she had happened to look at her breasts didn't necessarily mean that she'd wanted anything beyond an answer to her question about math. She herself had acted no better when she had ogled the woman from behind her sunglasses. She wondered how much more pleasant their conversation could have been if she hadn't jumped to conclusions about her intentions.

"What do you think, Sandy?" she asked as she stroked her cat's fur. Sandy purred and drooled, content to leave her to her inner turmoil.

Amy was out of practice at flirting and dating. This past year, she had been too focused on getting back in shape for lifeguard tryouts and then on working as a lifeguard to flirt or date. Her last several dates before that hadn't worked out very well either. They hadn't resulted in much more than a few hookups, perhaps because most of the women had sensed her discontent with her work at the auto dealership and quickly moved on.

A couple had lingered, but she knew that it had more to do with them liking her beachfront condo than Amy herself. She had learned that it was better not bring dates here, at least not at first, and instead go to their places. For the same reason, she rarely mentioned that she owned and managed an auto dealership and instead vaguely said that she worked at an auto dealership on the occasions that she was asked about work. She supposed that when it came to dating she'd become a bit jaded.

Her last actual relationship had been around the time of the startup of her dealership. She hadn't been able to devote much time and attention to the woman she was seeing then, and the relationship had foundered.

"I've got time now," she said aloud. When Sandy looked at her, she petted her head and sighed. Time enough, apparently, to sit home on a Saturday night and talk to the cat. Maybe it was time to try for a relationship again? That would entail dating again, of course, and hoping that it would lead to something more substantial and more satisfying than just one-night stands.

Sandy yawned, stretching her mouth open wide and enabling Amy to glimpse what looked like a red area around a tooth. "Oh, Sandy, what is that? Let me see that again."

She held her and gently pried her jaw open for another look. It wasn't easy, but when she did she saw an inflamed area around a tooth and got a big whiff of bad kitty breath.

She released Sandy, who jumped down to the floor and gave her a displeased look. "I know, Sweetie. I'm sorry." She went over to pet her soothingly. "But that tooth doesn't look good. I think a trip to the vet is in order." It had been a while since she had taken Sandy in, and she wasn't sure she still had the vet's number. She grabbed her phone off the side table to check. She'd do an Internet search if she didn't have it.

Her eyes widened when she saw an email notification on the screen. It was from the job application portal of the city of South Coast Beach, the website through which she had submitted her application for the instructor position with the junior lifeguard program. Had the hiring decisions been made? Her stomach was in her throat, but she didn't hesitate to tap to open the message.

"Yes! Got the job!" Amy let out a whoop of joy and jumped up and down. Her preparations and hard work were paying off, making the decision to take a break from her dealership that much more meaningful and the additional criticism likely to come from her family more bearable. She still had to find a buyer for her dealership, but she was so very excited about working in the junior lifeguard program that she would worry about that ever-present problem later. She already knew what her first duty as an instructor with the junior lifeguard program would be—working the tryouts next weekend!

Now about Sandy's tooth... Amy thumbed to her contact list for the vet.

CHAPTER FIVE

"It sure is crowded here," Sarah said, observing the rows of cars through the passenger window of Justin's car as he pulled into the parking lot of South Coast High School, where the junior lifeguard tryouts were being held. While he could have walked and had her meet him here, he had kindly driven to her house to pick her up.

"Yeah, this seems to be a popular place," he said with a smile. "Thanks again for coming here with me."

"No problem. It'll be fun to cheer on our students." Sarah paused. "But do you think it's okay that we're getting here with the event already part of the way through? We're probably going to miss some of our students. I don't want anyone to feel left out."

"I don't think it's anything to worry about. I only told mine I would stop by. Watching the whole thing would take most of the day. It should be fine to miss a couple of hours. And who knows if they'll even notice us in the audience? They'll be busy swimming."

"Okay, but let's try to make sure that we see some of both our seventh graders and eight graders."

"Yeah, that would probably be the best plan."

They found a parking space and made their way toward the sounds of splashing and cheering carrying from the school's outdoor swimming facility. Pausing inside the entrance, they took in the kids swimming in the eight lanes of the huge, sparkling, Olympic-size pool, the other excited kids on the sidelines, the enthusiastic crowd in the stands, and the handful of adults in red and white lifeguard uniforms.

Justin studied the posted signs for "Home" and "Visitors" and then turned to her. "Where should we sit?" he asked over the noise.

"Probably anywhere is fine, since it isn't an actual sporting competition."

"Okay, let's go over—" He looked past her shoulder. "Hi, Peter!" Justin smiled and waved.

She turned around to see Peter approaching with a friendly smile.

"Hi, I thought I recognized you both! Sarah and Justin, right? Nice to see you again." Peter shook their hands. Today, he was dressed in what Sarah recognized as a South Coast Beach lifeguard uniform of red shorts and a white polo shirt with the lifeguard emblem on it.

"It looks like you're working this gig," Justin said.

Peter chuckled good-naturedly. "I'm supervising today's tryouts. My junior lifeguard instructors are the ones running the show right now, though, so I was able to get away for a moment."

"In that case, do you have a second to tell us how this works?" Sarah asked. "Some of our students are swimming today, and we came by to cheer them on."

"That's really great," he said with a smile. "Hannah got here not long ago. I'm sure she and the others will be glad for your support." He paused. "As for how this works, we've got tryouts all weekend and then a few sessions during the week for people who couldn't make it this weekend. Today, we've got our younger kids swimming. Tomorrow will be high school-aged kids. Either way, what the kids have to do is complete a three-part swim test."

He gestured to the kids in the pool. "Right now, they're doing the 100-meter swim. It's noncompetitive, meaning that the kids are trying to beat the clock, not each other. If they succeed in swimming the distance within the given time frame, they move on to the next tests, which are swimming underwater without a breath for a certain distance and then treading water for a certain amount of time."

"Sounds tough," Sarah said.

"It's tough, but doable. We want to make sure everyone is able to swim well enough to be safe when we get them in the ocean for the program."

"Makes sense," Justin said. "Did we miss all of the seventh graders, or are some still swimming?"

"Actually, the kids swim on a first-come, first-served basis."

"Okay, great," Sarah said. "If each group can be a mixture of different grades, we'll see some of both levels of our students."

Peter nodded. "Speaking of that, there are a couple of other teachers here. They coach the swim team here at the high school, and they're helping us out with some of the facilities. If you want to join them, they're sitting over there." He pointed to a section of the stands.

Sarah turned to look. As soon as she saw the pair of teachers sitting there, one of whom was a young, good-looking man about their age, she knew what Justin's answer would be.

"That's fantastic," Justin said. "We weren't sure where to sit."

Why did he have all the luck finding potential dates? The gray-haired woman sitting with the man wasn't unattractive, but she looked to be about retirement age and therefore probably close to four decades older than Sarah. She hoped she would at least be pleasant to talk to while Justin flirted with the guy.

She walked over with Justin and they introduced themselves. The woman seemed friendly enough. Her name was Doris and she was a history teacher. Ron was an economics teacher. Sarah and Justin took seats in the row of bleacher seats with them as the next group of swimmers was getting into the pool.

Ron and Doris clapped for the swimmers, and Sarah and Justin joined in.

Justin turned to Sarah. "With the kids all in goggles and swim caps, I'm not sure I can tell who my students are."

"Me neither. I guess we can just cheer everyone on since they're really just racing against the clock, not each other."

"Works for me."

The kids were now lined up in the pool. When the lifeguard at the head of the pool blew the starting whistle, they kicked off the wall and started swimming. Sarah and Justin joined everyone in clapping and cheering again. Cries of "Go, go!" and "Kick, kick!" sounded from members of the crowd as the swimmers stroked freestyle down the length of the huge pool and back. When the laps were complete, the kids climbed out of the pool and got their times from the lifeguards on their lane, learning whether they had qualified to move on to the other swim tests. Several of them made fists of victory.

Justin was leaning over and chatting so much with Ron that Sarah made him change seats with her. She now sat by Doris and attempted to make conversation between the sessions. "How long have you been the swim coach?" she asked.

"Oh, I've been the coach for as long as I've been teaching here—almost too many years to count," Doris said with a laugh. "And long enough that a couple of the lifeguards working here today were on my swim teams."

"That must make you proud," Sarah said.

"Yes, yes it does," Doris nodded. "Those were also the years we won the regional swim championships and then went on to have winners in events at the state championships."

"That's very impressive," Sarah said.

"Thank you. As matter of fact, there's one of my state champs right over there." Doris pointed to a woman in red shorts, white polo shirt, wide-brimmed hat, and sunglasses who had bent over to help a young swimmer put on her swim cap.

Sarah stared, immediately recognizing her as the lifeguard she had talked to at the beach. She'd been too focused on chatting and trying to spot her students among the swimmers to notice her sooner. But now that she had, and even though she was wearing a hat and different attire this time, there was no mistaking that toned body or that beautiful face.

And the young swimmer that she was helping was Mandy! Sarah was careful not to play favorites with her students, but she couldn't help feeling a connection with a fellow Midwesterner. She mentally wished her luck today. As Sarah watched the lifeguard patiently demonstrate to her how to stretch the swim cap wide in order to put it on without pulling her hair and how to situate it to cover her ears, she felt herself smile. Once the cap was adjusted, the lifeguard straightened and pointed Mandy in the direction of a group of swimmers. Mandy thanked her and hurried off to join the others.

"Do you know Amy?" Doris asked, regarding Sarah with a curious expression.

Sarah blinked herself out of her daze. "Um, Amy?" Sarah repeated. Was that the woman's name? She liked it. "No, not really. I was at the beach last week and happened to ask her a question, but we didn't really...we don't really..."

She trailed off as the woman she now knew as Amy began to stride closer on those toned legs. She was coming over. Sarah wondered what Amy could want to say since their conversations seemed invariably to go badly. She hoped she wasn't upset about something again, but at the same time she looked forward to talking to her. Then again, she could be stopping by just to see Doris.

Before she knew it, Amy had climbed the stairs into the stands and stopped next to their row of bleacher seats. She removed her hat and ran a hand through her hair. Sarah wondered if her hair was as soft as it looked. She had another urge to run her hand through it. Then she remembered how difficult Amy had been last week and schooled her desires.

Amy gave a brief smile of acknowledgment to her former swim coach, whom she had no doubt chatted with earlier, and then faced Sarah. "Hi," she said with a smile. "I thought I recognized you again. I wanted to—"

"Wait a second—there isn't much room up here to talk," Sarah said, cutting her off in case she was going to rehash their awkward conversation from the tower. She didn't particularly want to do that in front of an audience. A glance at Justin and Ron informed her that they were so engrossed in their conversation with one another that they hadn't noticed anything, but Doris was still an audience who didn't need to hear any possible drama. "Why don't we go down there?" She gestured to the base of the stands and stood.

"Okay."

Excusing herself to Doris, Sarah stepped into the aisle where Amy was waiting. A pleasant feeling of heat rushed through her body when she slid past her to lead the way down the stairs. Keeping her desires in check was not working very well. She descended the stairs, Amy following. When they reached the bottom and moved out of way of the other spectators, she turned to face Amy. "What was it you wanted to say?"

Amy took a breath. "I wanted to apologize again for last week. I didn't mean to offend you."

"Okay," Sarah said. She accepted this apology, just as she had the one at the lifeguard tower, but she wasn't going to make this conversation easy for her. She was still stung by the brush-off that day.

"No, I mean it. I was rude—again."

"It's okay. You already apologized."

Amy pursed her lips as though unconvinced of Sarah's acceptance, but she seemed to recognize that she couldn't push the issue without seeming rude yet once again. Her lips were beautiful, and Sarah had to tear her gaze away. She wanted to be able to keep her wits about her this time.

"So, what are you doing here?" Amy asked.

Sarah frowned. Was she being accused of something? She had as much right to be here as the rest of the attendees. Was this the real reason Amy had wanted to talk to her? Had the offer of an apology only been a lead-in to an interrogation?

Maybe Amy had something against math teachers? Sarah gave in to the impulse to lay some more math talk on her and find out. "Maybe I came here today for a friendly discussion of formulas that might be used to calculate the volume of this pool," she said, sweeping her arm toward it.

Amy raised her eyebrows in surprise, and Sarah wished she could take back her deliberately provocative answer. It seemed Amy hadn't intended to be quarrelsome. Maybe her question had been innocuous, just as her own question at the lifeguard tower had been. Amy may only have asked why she was here out of curiosity and may not have been implying anything. Sarah opened her mouth to apologize and to tell her that she was here to cheer on her students, but Amy spoke first.

"Since this pool is rectangular and of constant depth, the question of which formula to use to calculate its volume would be a simple one." She quirked her lips into a teasing smile.

At the unexpected answer and smile, Sarah smiled in return. Maybe they could have a congenial conversation after all. "You're right. So maybe you aren't anti-math or sexist."

"What? Anti-math or sexist? Is that what you thought?"

Sarah shrugged. "Sure, I get it all the time, even from women. Some women have internalized sexism, believing like some men that girls can't do math."

Amy frowned. Whether the frown was in confusion over the idea itself or in disapproval of it, Sarah didn't know. "Just like some gay people have internalized homophobia," she continued.

Amy blinked. "The notion that girls can't do math is not an issue for me."

"Good," Sarah said.

"Nor is internalized homophobia, for that matter. I'm out and proud."

So, she *was* a lesbian. "Good to know." Sarah smiled. "So am I."

"Good to know, indeed," Amy said, smiling back warmly now. Sarah liked having that smile directed at her. "And just so you know," she continued, "algebra is not something I get asked about every day at the beach."

Sarah chuckled. "No, I suppose not. I didn't mean to throw you off your game that day," she teased.

Amy shook her head, chuckling too. She extended her hand. "I'm Amy. What's your name?"

"Sarah." She shook her hand, glad for the introduction despite already knowing her name and enjoying Amy's firm but gentle grip and the warmth of her touch.

"Pleased to meet you, Sarah," Amy said, releasing her hand.

Sarah's mind swirled, trying to reconcile the initial impression of Amy as ill-mannered and temperamental with the now friendly, not to mention appealingly astute, woman before her. It seemed too good to be true, kind of like Robin turned out to be.

Amy glanced toward the pool, and she did as well. Another group of swimmers was getting ready. Amy turned back to her. "I'd better get back to work, but I'd like the chance to get to know you better. Would you have coffee with me after today's tryouts are over?"

She took only a moment to contemplate the invitation; she wanted to get to know Amy better, too. "Yes. I think I'd like that." She smiled at her.

"Great." Amy smiled back. "I'll come back at the next break to make plans."

CHAPTER SIX

Sarah arrived slightly early at the coffeehouse that Amy had suggested. South Coast Beach Roasters was a coffeehouse that she knew well. It was near the beach and not far from her house, so she had walked. A few hours had passed since Justin had driven her home from the portion of the tryouts they had watched, but the event would only just have finished. Amy said she would come directly to the coffeehouse from it.

Sarah placed her drink order at the counter and took a seat at a table near the front windows, her nerves beginning to jump a bit as she thought about the date to come. Well, it was only really having coffee together. But if the lingering glances and smiles that she and Amy had shared this afternoon while making plans to meet here were any indication, it was a date too. She looked forward to chatting more with Amy, who, judging from her math quip about the pool, had hidden depths.

She hadn't been on many dates since her time with Robin, and none of them had been very fruitful, so she couldn't help being a little doubtful and wary now. Despite Amy's apologies, her sudden change of mood during their conversation at the tower last week was still fresh in her mind. She wasn't interested in dating a mercurial and difficult woman, even if that woman did have a body like Amy's. But Amy had been friendly enough today—charming, really. She hoped she had made the right choice to meet her to talk further.

When the barista called Sarah's name, she picked up her latte and then returned to her seat. Poised to take a sip, she saw Amy walk in. She set down her mug and gave a little wave to get her attention.

Amy's eyes lit up in recognition, and she made her way to the table. "Hi," she said, stopping before her and smiling.

"Hi," Sarah said, smiling also. For the first time since they'd met, Amy wasn't wearing her sunglasses, and Sarah found herself looking into a beautiful pair of golden-brown, agate-colored eyes.

"What are you drinking?" Amy asked.

"Hmm? Oh, um, a latte. I wanted to order something for you, too, but I wasn't sure what you might like."

"No problem. A latte sounds good, so let me go order one. I'll be right back."

Amy returned and joined Sarah at the small table. Despite having been able to watch and admire Amy a large part of the day at the pool, Sarah couldn't help letting her gaze drop to take in her figure once more. The polo shirt of her uniform hugged her breasts in a very appealing way, and the undone top button of the shirt allowed a tantalizing glimpse of the base of her throat and collarbones.

When Amy looked down at herself, Sarah realized she had let her gaze linger too long. "Oh, sorry about my uniform," Amy said. "Things at the tryouts ran a bit longer than anticipated, and I didn't change because I didn't want to be late."

Sarah shook her head. "No, it's fine. I didn't mean to stare—it's just that your uniform looks really great on you."

An expression of what might have been dismay flickered across Amy's face and confused Sarah. It was reminiscent of the suddenly cold reception she had been given last week at the tower.

The barista called Amy's order. Amy gave Sarah a wan smile before standing up to collect it.

Sarah wondered if she should get up and leave if they were going to have this much trouble communicating. But she wanted to know what the problem was, so she waited for Amy to return. When she sat back down, Sarah took a breath and faced her. "I can tell that what I said a moment ago upset you, even though it was a compliment. Was I too forward for you?"

Amy sighed and ran a hand through that silky-looking hair of hers. "No, no. It's fine. It's just... Sometimes I wonder if it's me that people are interested in or only the uniform or the swimsuit."

"Hmm," Sarah said. "I take that to mean you've had problems with people seeing the real you?" she asked.

"Yes, that's exactly what I mean."

"And not just seeing you as a hot lifeguard whose swimsuit fits her like a second skin?" Sarah arched an eyebrow.

Amy's lips twitched as she tried to hold back a smile. "Now *that* was forward."

Sarah smiled. "Was it welcome this time?"

Amy nodded and gave in to the smile.

Sarah put her elbow on the table and rested her chin in her hand in a show of further contemplating her. "Tell me, is this the reason for giving me the cold shoulder at your tower last week?"

"I wouldn't call it the 'cold shoulder' exactly..."

Sarah sat back and gave her a pointed look.

"Okay, maybe it was."

Sarah nodded emphatically, making her laugh. She liked hearing her laugh.

After a moment, Amy spoke. "I'm not trying to make excuses, but do you remember those guys in front of my tower?"

"The ones who were flexing and posing for you?"

"The same. Their antics were so tiresome. When you came up and asked your strange question, I thought it was just another ploy for attention. I'm sorry."

Sarah waved her hand. "You've apologized enough. I understand where you're coming from. I've had my share of attention-seeking students in classes over the years."

Amy nodded. "I can imagine."

Sarah's thoughts returned to their time at the beach and Justin's attempt to sell her on the finer points of a summer fling. She knew he wouldn't be able to stop himself from bringing it up at some point around Amy if this date turned into subsequent dates or anything more. He wouldn't do it to be mean, of course, but he would enjoy gloating that he was right. As it was, when Amy had returned to the stands today to arrange their coffee date and Justin realized who she was, his eyes had almost bugged out of his head. Sarah didn't want him to say something about their fling talk and have Amy take it the wrong way. She wondered if she should mention it now herself and get it over with, even if it might make Amy suspicious of her intentions again.

"Is something the matter?" Amy asked.

She looked up, realizing that she had been staring down at the table and chewing her lip. Sometimes she wished she wasn't so easy to read. "No, nothing is the matter. It's just that...in the interest of full disclosure..."

"This doesn't sound good," Amy said with a nervous laugh.

She sighed. "Yeah. It's just that my friend Justin—the one you met—told me that day at the beach that I should have a summer fling."

"Oh." Amy sat back. "And what did you say?"

"I reminded him that flings aren't really my thing."

"So that isn't why you approached me?"

"No," Sarah said. "I'm a little too shy for that. Well, not shy, necessarily, but let's just say I'm not as bold as that. I really did only come up to get more information for my students." At Amy's skeptical look, she gave a shrug and added, "But I'm only human and not above flirting. Given the choice, I would rather approach a lifeguard who looks like you."

Amy quirked a smile at that, and Sarah was glad. But she remained silent, as if waiting for her to continue. "Am I missing something?" She broke the silence.

Sarah frowned. "What? No, I told you everything."

"Then I guess I'm confused, because it doesn't sound like there was much of anything to disclose."

Sarah relaxed at the realization that Amy wasn't bothered by the fling conversation. "I just thought it would be better if you heard it now so you wouldn't get the wrong idea if it came up later."

"Oh," Amy said with a nod. "Can I tell you something?" she asked, leaning forward.

"Okay," Sarah said, meeting Amy's beautiful eyes.

"I wasn't fully immune to your charms that day, either."

"No?" Sarah smiled.

"No. The flexing and posing of those guys in front of my tower may have been wasted on me, but your short shorts were not wasted on me at all," Amy said, a smile tugging at her lips. "Nor was your very lovely face."

Sarah felt herself blush. "Now who's being forward?" she asked. Still a little embarrassed, she looked down at the table. Noticing the latte she had all but forgotten, she picked it up and took a sip.

Amy sipped her own drink. "So, you never said what brought you to the junior lifeguard tryouts?"

This time, Sarah didn't feel criticized by the question. "Justin and I were there to cheer on our students."

Amy smiled. "That was nice of you. How do you know Doris?"

"I don't. Or, I didn't until today. Peter suggested we sit with her and Ron since they're teachers too. And before you can ask, we know Peter because he's the uncle of Hannah, one of our students. Don't worry. I'm not stalking you." Sarah softened the last comment with a smile.

"Sorry, I didn't mean to sound like I was interrogating you."

"It's all right. If I were you, I'd have been curious, too." She explained how she and Justin had run into Hannah and Peter at the Earth Day cleanup. "By the way, how did Hannah end up doing?" she asked. She and Justin had only seen the first portion of her swim test. Sarah had seen Mandy and another student qualify but wasn't sure about the others.

"Hannah passed all three parts of the test with flying colors."

"That's great."

Amy nodded. "Peter is one proud uncle." She took another sip of her latte and then set it down, leaving her hand wrapped around the mug.

Sarah sipped her own latte, her gaze lingering on Amy's hand that cupped the mug. Recalling the warmth of her handshake earlier in the day, she wondered what her warm hand would feel like cupping her breast, her hip, her…

"Are you okay?" Amy asked. "You look a little flushed."

She blinked and took a breath. "Now that you mention it, I do feel a little warm." She searched for an excuse. "Maybe I should have had an iced latte."

"Let me get you some water." Amy got up. "Be right back."

Sarah watched Amy as she walked across the room to the water dispenser. She was sexy just filling a glass of water. Not wanting to be caught staring again, she made herself look away before she returned.

"Here you go." Amy placed the glass of water in front of her.

"Thanks." She took a sip and closed her eyes briefly as the cool liquid refreshed her. When she opened them, she found Amy gazing at her.

"Better?" Amy asked.

Sarah swallowed hard. "Better."

"Well, well," a woman's voice intruded. "What do we have here?"

Sarah turned to see Robin standing alongside their table and looking from her to Amy. She hadn't seen her ex-girlfriend enter the coffeehouse, so caught up had she been in Amy.

Robin appeared to be scrutinizing Amy's lifeguard uniform. She was dressed smartly as usual, like the high-powered real estate agent she was, and wearing the watch that Sarah had always thought probably cost as much as her own car. She held two coffees to go. One of the coffees was probably for a client, as Robin was not in the habit of frequenting independent coffeehouses. Apparently done scrutinizing Amy, Robin turned her attention to Sarah. "Dating someone of your own social class? Maybe it's for the best." Without waiting for a response, she turned and walked to the door.

"What...?" Amy looked at Sarah, frowning. She turned toward Robin's retreating figure. "Hey..." She started to get up, but Sarah laid her hand on her arm. She hesitated but sat back down, watching her exit the coffeehouse. She looked at Sarah again.

Sarah sighed. "That was Robin—my ex."

Amy raised her eyebrows. "I can see why."

"Yeah." Sarah watched through the window as Robin slid into her double-parked Mercedes-Benz S-Class sedan with her coffees and drove away. "If I never date another stuck-up rich woman again it will be too soon."

Amy blinked and looked away. Sarah wondered at her odd reaction, wondered what she was thinking, since it was clear that dating Robin hadn't been a particularly good choice on her part. Amy looked at her and seemed about to speak but then closed her mouth.

"It's okay," Sarah spoke into the silence.

"Okay? Your ex? No, that definitely wasn't okay," she said, shaking her head.

She sighed again. "Yeah, I know. That's why she's my ex. I still get mad at myself for even having had a relationship with her."

"I hate to ask," Amy said, "but I can't help wondering. Why did you?"

"Believe it or not, she can be charming. It wasn't all bad. That, and you saw her clothes, her car. I'm embarrassed to say that the lifestyle I had a taste of with her made me overlook some of the times when she was less charming. As I said, I'm not going to do that again." Sarah looked down at the table. Amy was silent, no doubt wondering how she could have made such bad dating choices.

Just as the silence was becoming uncomfortable, Amy reached over and patted her arm comfortingly. "Don't be so tough on yourself. What happened to you could happen to anyone."

She wasn't convinced, but Amy's touch felt nice. She didn't want to talk about her ex any longer. She took another sip of the cool water that Amy had brought her, wishing that she would gaze at her again like she had before Robin had so rudely appeared. What had she been thinking about at that moment? From her expression, she had an inkling it might have been something along the lines of her own contemplation of what Amy's warm hands might feel like on her body. Unfortunately, Sarah was seeing only a distant look in her eyes now. She searched for a new topic of conversation. "So how did you pick this coffeehouse?"

"What?" Amy asked, seeming taken aback. "I had no idea your ex would be here."

"No..." she said in dismay. "That's not what I meant." It seemed that Amy was back to taking offense at simple questions. She put her head in her hands and felt tears gathering, which dismayed her further. She was so frustrated with the way things with Amy had deteriorated after Robin had blighted the day and was still embarrassed by her naïveté with Robin. She took a breath and, blinking the tears away before they could fall, looked at Amy. "I only was asking because I live nearby, and I wondered if maybe you chose this place because you live nearby, too."

"Oh. I'm sorry. I guess I sounded defensive. But your ex— Robin, was it? —kind of got my hackles up."

"Sorry."

"No, don't be. It's not your fault."

Sarah sniffled.

"And don't let her upset you. I hope you won't be offended if I say she's obviously not worth getting upset over."

She took a breath. "Yeah. You're right."

Amy nodded briskly, as if the matter of Robin were settled. "So, you were saying that you live near this coffeehouse?"

"Yes. Not on my own, unfortunately. I have roommates. But they're nice. They're at work at the hospital today. I walked here." Realizing that her lingering embarrassment was causing her to blather, she stopped talking. At least the return to their previous conversation was helping the tears dissipate. She sniffled once more.

Amy squeezed her hand and smiled. "You're adorable."

Sarah wasn't sure what was adorable about her rambling answer or sniffling, but she was glad that Amy was smiling again. It made her smile, too. Though her smile might have been brighter if she hadn't ignored her question about whether she also lived nearby. Was her living situation another of her issues? Sarah had no idea, but she was running low on patience. Why was Amy so nice sometimes, yet so unreachable at other times?

Maybe Justin was right. Maybe summer wasn't the time to think about relationships. Maybe summer was the time to consider a fling. Relationships hadn't been working out, and a fling could be refreshing, like he'd said. Having a fling would be a departure from the usual for her, but for a woman with a body like Amy had, she was willing to venture into the unknown. Unfortunately, it seemed like Amy might not be into flings since she seemed to have such hang-ups about people admiring her body and her uniform. She sighed.

"Maybe we should get out of here," Amy said.

Sarah looked at her in surprise. Surely she hadn't read her mind.

She seemed to read her surprise. "Um, I didn't mean it like that. I just thought that you might want to get some fresh air after—no offense—" She waved her hand vaguely at the area where Robin had been standing. "You know, your ex. Go for a walk, maybe?"

"A walk sounds great. Some fresh air would be nice." She pushed back her chair and stood.

Amy opened the door for Sarah, and they left the coffeehouse and began strolling down the sidewalk.

Amy wondered if her suggestion that they get out of there had been a Freudian slip. She was beginning to think that the fling Sarah had spoken of earlier wouldn't be too off base from what they would be able to have, because it didn't seem like they were going to be able to date or have a relationship. Not if Sarah was so easily seduced by material possessions.

Amy had already dated a couple of women like that. She didn't want it to happen again, which was why she was in the habit of keeping quiet about her beachfront condo and her luxury auto dealership.

On the other hand, Sarah had said that she didn't want to date another rich woman. Did that mean she was put off by wealth now? Amy had almost said that not all wealthy women were like Robin, but she wouldn't have been able to explain such a comment very well without revealing a lot more of herself than she normally liked to do this early. She didn't think her own finances were in Robin's league, but she did have a certain amount of money. It was beginning to look like this coffee date was not a very auspicious foray back into the dating world.

It didn't help that Sarah had asked where she lived. She couldn't win by answering that question, given Sarah's mixed messages. If she mentioned her wealth, she ran the risk of her glomming onto her and hoping to move into her beachfront condo as a couple of other women had tried to do. Then again, she might be repelled because of her experiences with Robin.

Any way she looked at it, she saw a problem. Sarah was either going to be overly interested in her or not interested at all. Neither sounded good.

But Amy wasn't ready to let go of a woman with a body like Sarah's, with its luscious curves. She looked even prettier today than she had at the beach. Her long blond hair was down, instead of up in a loose ponytail, and it fell in gentle golden waves to rest on a wide-necked knit top instead of a running shirt. She had on light makeup: a little eye shadow that brought out her lovely brown eyes and lipstick that accentuated her very kissable lips.

If dating wasn't going to be feasible because of whatever implication Amy's financial status would have for Sarah, maybe a fling with her was the answer. She could have some fun and wait a little longer to venture back into the dating world. Flings weren't usually her style, but maybe she could make an exception. She wouldn't need to part with too many personal details that way and might be able to avoid the topic of money all together. The only problem was, Sarah had said she wasn't into flings. Amy sighed.

"So, what about you? Do you live nearby, too?" Sarah asked as they walked, repeating her earlier question.

Amy wanted to answer but didn't see how she could without either an outright lie or revealing more than she wanted to. And she didn't want to lie any more than she already had with omissions. "Um…"

"Never mind. You don't have to tell me," Sarah said, shaking her head.

"I want to tell you. It's just that it's complicated."

"Does that mean you live with an ex-girlfriend?" Sarah asked.

"No."

"A current girlfriend?"

"No."

"Then it's not too complicated for me," Sarah said. Amy wondered at Sarah's newly matter-of-fact tone of voice during the questions; it was almost like she was trying to make a decision of some sort.

"A boyfriend?"

Amy turned her head to stare at her. "No."

Sarah laughed. "Just checking."

Amy shook her head. Boyfriend, indeed. But at least Sarah's good spirits seemed to have returned.

"You don't have to tell me about any of it until you're ready," Sarah said.

Amy didn't want her to get her hopes up, so she just nodded. As they continued their walk, she was a little surprised that Sarah didn't press the issue. She could only imagine what she must be thinking about her statement that it was complicated. Why did things have to be so difficult? They walked in silence for a bit, on a residential street now, and Amy admired some of the cute houses.

"I have another question," Sarah announced. She slowed, taking hold of one of Amy's hands to slow her as well.

"Yes?" she asked, hoping that it would be a question that she could answer and not another that she would have to sidestep.

Sarah brought them to a stop in the middle of the sidewalk and turned to face her. She took a breath as though gathering her courage, making Amy brace herself for what she would say.

"Would having a fling really be such a bad idea?" she asked.

The question still caught Amy off guard. What had caused Sarah to revisit the idea of a fling? She couldn't be sure, but she knew herself well enough to be aware that she had been probably sending her own mixed messages with her hot and cold behavior and non-answers. She could see how that would make her seem like bad dating material.

The good news was that, like her, Sarah apparently was unable to ignore their physical attraction. Just the feel of Sarah's hand that continued to hold hers was causing a wonderful warmth to suffuse her body. She looked at Sarah's lips, wanting very much to claim her mouth with her own and to do the same with the rest of her beautiful body, for that matter.

"No, actually, I don't think a fling would be such a bad idea at all."

Sarah smiled, her gaze dropping to Amy's lips, before returning to her eyes. "Good," she said, gesturing to the adjacent house, "because this is where I live, and I'd like you to come in."

CHAPTER SEVEN

Buzzing with arousal from the hungry look Amy had given her in return, Sarah let them into her house and then turned to close and lock the front door. Her hands shook a little from her excitement, not to mention her nervousness. She had surprised herself at being bold enough to invite Amy in. She was also surprised that Amy had agreed to come in, given her earlier complaints about being wanted only for her body or her uniform.

Amy's thoughts must have changed during this date, just as Sarah's had. Either that or hooking up was all that Amy had wanted in the first place and she had been putting on airs earlier. She was so confusing. But she was also very, very hot, and Sarah planned to thoroughly enjoy her body. Turning around, she faced her. Before she could so much as plan her next move, Amy's mouth was on hers.

Amy's kiss was hungry, and Sarah liked it. She slid her arms around Amy's shoulders and returned the kiss with a hunger of her own. Amy moaned, wrapping her arms around her and pulling her closer. Sarah opened her mouth to her, and Amy's tongue met hers, circling, sucking, sending pleasure through her, and only stopping when they both needed to catch their breath. Amy's eyes were filled with heat, her lips still parted after the kiss. It made Sarah's center throb.

"I want you," Amy said.

"I want you, too."

Amy backed her against the wall. "I want you here, now," she breathed and began kissing along her neck.

Sarah tilted her head back and moaned at the delicious feel of Amy's warm lips and tongue on her neck. She threaded the fingers of one hand through her hair, cupping the back of her head. Her hair was just as wonderfully soft as it looked.

Amy licked and gently nipped the sensitive skin at the base of her neck and around her collarbones until she reached the boundaries of her shirt. "Let's get this shirt off." She grasped the hem and stepped back enough to pull it up and off Sarah and then toss it aside. Her hands immediately went to Sarah's nipples, which were pushing at the fabric of her bra. She thumbed them and Sarah let out another moan. Amy reached around and unclasped the bra. Sarah shrugged out of it, and it fell to the floor.

Amy gazed at her bare breasts with lustful appreciation before bending forward to roll her tongue around and over a hardened nipple. Sarah arched with another moan. When Amy moved to the other breast, giving it the same attention, she clutched at Amy's shoulders, arching her pelvis into her for more contact.

"Let's get the rest of this off," Amy said urgently. She reached for the button of Sarah's capri pants.

"Yes," Sarah said breathlessly, but she caught Amy's hands. She wasn't going to be the only one undressed when she so badly wanted to see Amy's body. "I've got this. You have some catching up to do." She arched an eyebrow and moved her eyes over Amy's still fully clothed figure.

Amy hastily unbuttoned her polo shirt and pulled it over her head. She shucked off the rest of her clothes and her shoes with the same rapidity.

Mesmerized, Sarah forgot all about undoing her capris and openly admired the athletic physique of the woman before her. She drank it all in: the softly muscled shoulders and arms, the lightly defined abdomen, the toned thighs and calves. Swimsuit tan lines highlighted Amy's torso, making her full breasts stand out in creamy relief to the rest of her tanned body. "You're beautiful," Sarah said.

Amy smiled. "I think you're beautiful, too. And I want to see the rest of you." She advanced toward her and reached for the capris again, unbuttoning and unzipping. Sarah stepped out of her sandals and wriggled out of her capris and undies.

"Yes, very beautiful," Amy said, gazing at her. She pulled her close and kissed her long and deep.

Sarah surrendered to the scorching kiss, the full length of Amy's solid but soft body pressed against her. She backed toward the wall again for support. When Amy broke the kiss, Sarah was breathless. "Your kisses…they're driving me wild." Arousal was already slicking her thighs. "I need you—soon." She grasped Amy's shoulders and hooked a leg around her hip, pressing her swollen, wet center against her.

Amy let out a little growl of pleasure. She pressed closer, taking some of Sarah's weight and gripping the thigh that encircled her hip, supporting it and caressing it, while bending to kiss and lightly bite one of her shoulders. When she unleashed her tongue on her nipples again, Sarah moaned and clutched at her back. Amy's hand moved closer to where she needed it. Sarah gasped as her fingers found her swollen folds.

"Is this okay?" Amy asked.

"Very okay," Sarah breathed, her center aching with need. She kissed Amy urgently.

Amy stroked her fingers through Sarah's wetness, brushing her clitoris.

"Ohhh," Sarah moaned.

Amy set her feet and legs to more fully support Sarah and pressed her fingers into Sarah's liquid heat.

"Oh, yes," Sarah said as Amy entered her. She allowed herself to relax into Amy's sure stance, taking in the full length of her fingers.

"You're so wet, and you feel so good," Amy said, her breath warm against Sarah's neck.

"Mmm," Sarah said, enjoying every sensation of Amy filling her.

Amy began to move, setting a steady rhythm of pulling back to near withdrawal only to change course and enter again.

"Oh…oh, yes!" Sarah felt her swollen folds and clitoris swell further with each stroke. It all felt so good. Her breath started to come in hard gasps and Amy gave her faster, firmer strokes. Sarah gave a last cry as a powerful orgasm racked her body. She melted against Amy, breathless.

Amy quickly repositioned herself, pressing her swollen wetness against Sarah's upper thigh. Sarah tightened her arms around her, pulling her closer. "Yes, let me feel you."

Amy rolled her hips, rocking her hard, slickened clitoris against Sarah. "Yes," Sarah said, moving one of her hands to her buttocks, pulling her even closer. Amy rolled her hips faster, her breath becoming ragged until, at last, she let out a cry and dropped her head against Sarah's shoulder. "So good…" she murmured.

"Yes…so good," Sarah said. She held Amy while her breathing slowed. "Let's go lie down. I don't know about you, but I need to recover before round two."

Amy straightened with a soft chuckle. "Yeah, me too."

Sarah took her hand and led her to her bedroom.

* * *

In the cool evening air, Amy walked back to the coffeehouse to pick up her car. Sarah had offered to drive her, but she had declined, encouraging her to stay comfy in bed for a while longer since the coffeehouse was only a short distance away.

Amy wished that was her only reason for declining. The other reason had to do with the fact that her vehicle was a luxury SUV and such a vehicle was either going to be repulsive to Sarah with its implications of wealth or trigger excessive interest on her part. Amy still didn't know which, but both options were worrisome because she didn't want to create problems with Sarah when their fling was off to such a good start.

It was better to just keep things simple by walking. But walking wasn't simple either; Sarah had insisted that Amy take a sweatshirt to wear against the chill of the marine air. Amy had complied, and while she was grateful for the warmth, it felt very intimate to wear Sarah's shirt, even when taking into account the intense physical intimacy that they had just shared.

No, keeping things simple was not going to be an easy feat. The feel of Sarah answering her hungry kisses, the press of her body against her own, the sensation of gliding her fingers through her hot wetness, the sounds of her pleasure… Amy couldn't remember anyone ever having made her so hard, so wet. And the second time, amazingly, had been as fantastic as the first. Amy was aroused again just thinking about the tantalizing things that Sarah had done to her body in the bedroom. She could barely wait to return next weekend. How was a fling going to be enough with such a passionate, responsive, and kind lover?

Amy neared the coffeehouse. She had parked in a two-hour zone. If she had gotten a ticket for exceeding the time limit, it would be well worth it. She grinned when she saw her vehicle—there was no ticket on the windshield. She unlocked her door and got in. The feminine scent from Sarah's sweatshirt enveloped her in the enclosed space. The scent was something floral and a little bit sweet, like freesias. She inhaled deeply, breathing in Sarah's fragrance, before starting her SUV and heading home.

Sarah lingered in bed. Her limbs were languid, her body was satiated, but her mind was busy. She had offered Amy a ride back to the coffeehouse to pick up her car, but she had demurred, suggesting that Sarah relax in the bed for a while longer. When Sarah pointed out that it was almost dark outside and that the temperature had become a little brisk for Amy to walk in her shorts and polo shirt, she had still demurred, saying that the coffeehouse wasn't very far. At least she had accepted a sweatshirt to wear.

Sarah had tried not to read too much into all of it, but she couldn't help wondering if there was another reason for her refusal. It wasn't anything to do with the sex, because the second time had been just as delicious as the first and they had already made plans for her to come over again next weekend.

The more Sarah pondered the issue, the more she wondered if Amy's refusal of a ride to the coffeehouse had something to do with her car. Maybe she was embarrassed of it just as she seemed to be embarrassed of her living situation, wherever it was that she lived. Maybe she didn't want Sarah to see her car, just like she didn't want her to know where she lived.

Sarah didn't know how Amy's car could be much worse than her own old beat-up sedan, but maybe it was. Maybe she thought it would be a turnoff. Didn't Amy realize that she couldn't turn Sarah off if she tried? The level of arousal and want that Sarah had experienced with Amy was not one she had experienced before. How was a fling going to be enough with such a passionate, considerate, and intuitive lover?

Sarah didn't know how much money lifeguards made, but maybe Amy's finances were stretched thin. That didn't matter to Sarah, but maybe it mattered to Amy. She wished Amy knew there was no need to be ashamed of her living situation or of her car.

CHAPTER EIGHT

It was the Saturday of the Fun Run fundraiser for the SCB junior lifeguard program. When Sarah heard Justin pull his car into her driveway to pick her up as anticipated, she went outside to greet him.

Justin stepped out of his car, leaving the engine running. "Hi. Are you still sure you want to walk to the check-in? We could just drive."

"Yeah—you know how bad parking is by the pier. It's probably even worse today. If we don't get a good spot, we could end up walking from somewhere this far anyway."

"That's true." He got back in, shut off the engine, and joined her in the driveway. "There's always plenty of parking for me here with your roommates gone all the time."

"That there is." Fiona and Susie were at work again this weekend. "Are you ready to go?"

He nodded. "I am."

They began walking to the beach.

"It's probably good to walk anyway," Justin said. "I think we need a thorough warm-up. I saw Marsha in the teachers' lounge on Friday, and after talking to her, I got the impression that this Fun Run is more competitive than we think."

"Uh-oh," Sarah said. She already harbored doubts about whether their sporadic bouts of jogging the past few weeks had been enough preparation. "What exactly did she say?"

"She said something about not wanting to get run over by anyone with a baby stroller this year."

Sarah laughed and gave Justin a shove on the shoulder. "Oh, come on. Don't joke. You had me worried there for a minute."

"No, I'm not joking. She said that the people pushing the jogging strollers are some of the most hardcore racers. Apparently, one of the strollers nipped her ankle last year."

"Ankle-nipping baby strollers? And on the sand, no less?"

Justin shrugged. "She said they have wheels as big as a kid's bicycle wheels."

Sarah blinked. "Hmm. Let's steer clear of those then."

"Yeah, I think we're going to be sore enough after running these three miles even without getting our ankles nipped."

"Probably, but at least it's for a good cause."

"And how is your lifeguard, by the way?"

She drew in a breath, uncertain as to how to answer.

"Not good?" he asked, frowning.

"No, it's not that…"

"Well, what is it then? Oh, wait, I get it. Did you end up with a wine spritzer instead of a rosé?"

"What?" She looked at him and then rolled her eyes. "Oh, no, not another wine analogy." But she couldn't resist. "Okay, I'll bite—what do you mean this time?"

He shrugged. "Just that things can fizz out."

She groaned. "Oh, boy. You are so cheesy."

"What?" he said, sounding slightly indignant. "A spritzer after the bubbles wear off is no fun."

She shook her head.

"So, tell me what's going on," he prodded.

Sarah sighed. "Things fizzing out isn't the problem. On the contrary, things are very lively." Images of Amy came to her: Amy's eyes dark with desire, Amy's hot tongue on one of her breasts, Amy moving between her thighs… They had spent two amazing Saturdays in a row together now. Things were very lively. "But I don't know… I guess I just get the sense that she's holding something back."

"Something personal, you mean?" he asked.

"Yeah, something personal."

"Well, it *is* a fling. Maybe she doesn't want to get too involved."

"You might be right, but I wish I knew what was on her mind. We're good together. It feels like we could have something more, if not for whatever is holding her back."

"It's okay to want something more."

"That's what I think."

"That's the spirit." He bumped her shoulder. "Something more serious and robust, something like a cabernet sauvignon."

Sarah laughed and looked over at him. "I think you've missed your calling. You should have been a sommelier."

"Nah. I've just been wined and dined a lot."

"And how is Ron? Does he wine and dine you well?" Sarah asked. Justin had really seemed to connect with the economics teacher at the tryouts two weeks ago.

"Yes, he does. We tried a new restaurant just a couple nights ago."

"Was it any good?"

"The food was so-so, but it was a good date anyway. He said he'd cook for me next time, which is actually today. He invited me over for lunch after the Fun Run."

"Ah-ha! Now I've got this all figured out," Sarah said, pointing her finger teasingly at Justin. "You're planning to run extra fast this morning so that you can get to your lunch date sooner—that's why you're convinced we're going to be so sore after the run."

"Now that you mention it, running faster is a good idea," he teased her back.

She laughed and then paused. "But seriously, I'm glad it's going well between you two." She bumped his shoulder. "Maybe the relationship has aging potential, like that cabernet sauvignon you mentioned."

He laughed, and she tossed him another smile, trying to set aside her preoccupation about whether her time with Amy would be able to become more than a fling. What they had right now was enough, she told herself. Amy was working in her tower today, and Sarah looked forward to running by during the event this morning.

After she and Justin arrived at the pier, they checked in for the run and received their participant numbers. Affixing the numbers to their shirts, they joined the crowd of other registrants on the beach in the area behind the starting line. Some of the people assembled were stretching and bending, getting ready to run. Others were milling about or looking at a display of lifeguard vehicles and equipment. It looked like there were hundreds of runners, which was good news for the junior lifeguard program because the Fun Run would probably raise several thousand dollars.

It was easy to spot the more serious runners in the crowd. Sarah observed a particularly intense bout of stretching being done by a lean man with a baby stroller that not only had extra-large, extra-wide, extra-nubby tires but also looked like it had shock absorbers. Sarah planned to steer a wide berth from that industrial-grade stroller. The only nips she wanted to feel anywhere on her body were the occasional playful ones that Amy gave her. She hadn't spotted Marsha, their colleague who had warned of such strollers, but supposed that she was in the crowd somewhere getting ready to race, too.

A man in a lifeguard uniform walked toward the lifeguard truck that was parked some distance in front of the crowd. "Hey, is that Peter?" Sarah asked, pointing toward him when she had Justin's attention.

Justin craned his neck trying to see around the crowd. The man was getting into the truck. "Yeah, I think so," he said. "Maybe that's going to be a pace car."

The light bar on the truck started flashing. "Must be almost race time." Sarah pressed forward with Justin and the rest of the crowd.

The signal was given, and they took off with the rest of the runners. With the excitement and adrenaline of the start, people ran fast. Soon though, everyone settled into their individual paces, and the crowd began to spread out. Jogging alongside one another, Sarah and Justin passed one lifeguard tower, then another, the lifeguards at each standing on deck and cheering on all of the runners. Sarah looked into the distance toward Amy's tower. She ran faster.

"Hey, wait up," Justin said between breaths.

"I thought you were hungry for your lunch with Ron," she challenged him.

Grinning, he picked up the pace.

The crowd around them spread out further the farther they went. Sarah and Justin neared the stretch of beach in front of Amy's tower. Amy was standing on the deck, clapping and cheering as people passed. Sarah put on an extra burst of speed.

Justin matched her new pace and, panting, said, "Apparently, I'm not the only one who's hungry."

She grinned at him. It was true—she did want to impress Amy. Could Amy see them now that they had put more space between themselves and the other runners? Sarah waved over to the tower just to make sure. Her heart lifted when Amy waved back. It was such a better experience than the first time she had approached the tower those few weeks ago.

She and Justin were now running fast enough that they passed more of the other runners and Sarah didn't think she imagined it when Amy clapped and cheered more loudly. The best part of the Fun Run was that it looped back to the pier, so she would get to pass Amy's tower again.

* * *

After the run, Sarah and Justin walked back to Sarah's house. Even though her legs were tired, the walk home was a nice cool-down. In the driveway, Sarah waited while Justin unlocked his car.

He turned to her before getting in. "I don't know about you, but I'm going to be feeling that run for few days."

"Me, too. We might have overdone it a little."

"We?"

She laughed. "Yeah, but we ran really well." She put her hand up to give him a high-five. They had run the entire distance without walking and had placed respectably among the crowd of participants.

He smiled and met her hand with a friendly slap. "Yeah, we did."

She said goodbye and he drove off to get ready for his lunch date with Ron. Looking forward to a shower, she went inside the house and into the bathroom. She turned on the water to heat up, peeled off her running clothes, and stepped under the warm spray. It felt wonderful on her tired muscles.

She wished she had a lunch date like Justin and Ron did. All she and Amy did was meet here at her house. Tonight would be the third Saturday in a row. Not that she was complaining about their time in bed. There was nothing to complain about there, but it would be nice to go out sometime or to Amy's place. But she knew that Amy wasn't her girlfriend and that she wasn't Amy's girlfriend. That was what she had signed up for when she decided to have a fling. That was how these things worked, after all.

Today at the beach, though, it had almost felt like Amy *was* her girlfriend—watching her do the charity run, cheering for her, waving to her. It made her feel special, not like she was just someone's fling. It was why she preferred dating and relationships over casual hookups. She didn't know if she could continue with their current arrangement much longer. She just didn't think she was cut out for it, even if the sex was amazing.

She finished showering and then toweled off. Her ruminations hadn't solved anything, including the problem of lunch. She was hungry and didn't feel like cooking. She wanted to go out.

She wished Fiona and Susie were here. She liked it when they all went out to eat, especially when it was in Little Saigon. Going there meant driving a couple of cities over to the city of Westminster, but it was worth it to eat at Susie's favorite Vietnamese restaurant. Sarah salivated just thinking of the restaurant's spicy stir-fried scallop and rice noodle dish. Right now, though, she was too hungry to drive so far.

Maybe today would be a good day to try the Vietnamese food truck that had recently started parking near the beach. While it was doubtful it would have the same scallop and noodle dish, it should have other tasty choices. She got dressed.

When she reached the food truck, she stepped off her bicycle and locked it to a post. Bicycling had required some effort so soon after the Fun Run, but parking her bike was a lot easier than parking her car around here. Two women were working in the truck, one preparing the food and one handling customers at the window. From age and resemblance, she guessed that the women might be mother and daughter.

She joined the line at the truck's window and read the posted handwritten menu while she waited. It looked like the truck offered many of her favorites, but she decided to try only simple items first to see what the food was like. When it was her turn to order, the older of the two Vietnamese women smiled down at her from the window.

"Xin chào," Sarah said in greeting.

The woman's smile broadened. "Xin chào."

In Vietnamese, Sarah ordered a steamed pork bun and a large bowl of chicken phở. The soup of rich broth, rice noodles, sliced chicken, and cilantro was a favorite. She was tempted to also get the green papaya salad, another favorite, but decided to wait until next time. The pork bun and soup would be enough since she and Justin had had a complimentary snack from the refreshment table at the Fun Run.

The woman gave her the total in Vietnamese. Sarah didn't know many numbers in the language, so she looked to the cash register display for the amount she owed. She took a bill out of the pocket in her shorts and paid. The woman gave her the change and thanked her.

"Cảm ơn," Sarah thanked her also.

A voice behind Sarah said, "I'm no expert, but those Vietnamese intonations of yours sound pretty authentic."

Sarah turned around and found herself face to face with a smiling Amy. Sarah smiled back. "Hi."

"Hi."

"What are you doing here?"

"I'm on my lunch break. I was going to order a sandwich. Can I join you?"

"Of course."

Amy stepped to the window and ordered a chicken bánh mì and an iced tea. Sarah also liked those chicken sandwiches with pickled vegetables, thinly sliced chiles, and sprigs of cilantro. Amy moved to the side next to her to wait for their food. "So, you speak Vietnamese?" Amy asked.

"Just enough for basic greetings and to order some food. One of my roommates is Vietnamese and I've picked up a few words from her when we go out to eat."

"That's neat."

The woman called their orders. They collected their food and found a bench nearby to sit and eat at. As they ate, they chatted about the Fun Run. Some of the julienned carrots and daikon fell from Amy's sandwich onto the wrapper in her lap. She gathered them up and tilted her head back before dropping them into her mouth.

Sarah's eyes followed the exposed line of her neck, the gentle curve of it reminding her of how Amy had looked during climax the last time Sarah had her in her mouth.

"What?" Amy asked, but her crooked grin told her she might have some idea of what Sarah was thinking.

"Nothing," Sarah said, smiling back. She was enjoying herself; this lunch felt almost like a date. Could she ask Amy a question without her closing up as she was prone to doing? She decided to start with something benign. "What have you been doing this week outside of work?" She did her best to keep her tone casual.

"I took my cat to the vet," Amy said after a moment.

"I didn't know you had a cat." Sarah was unable to stop herself from blurting the obvious. There were so many simple things she didn't know about her. Learning that she had a pet was at least a start. "Was something the matter with your cat? Or was the visit just for a checkup?"

"I noticed something going on with her tooth, so I took her in last week to have it examined. The vet said it was infected and needed to be pulled, so I took her in again this week for that."

"Is she doing okay?"

"Yes. I know Sandy—that's her name—is better because she's not drooling like she used to."

"That's good," Sarah said.

Amy nodded. "I'm so glad she's well. I feel bad for not realizing something was wrong sooner. She's older and I guess I should take her in for checkups more often, but she hates being put in a cat carrier and the dogs in the waiting room always scare her so much that she's skittish for days afterward."

Sarah nodded. She remembered accompanying her mother on a few stressful visits to the vet with the family dogs and cats over the years. She also remembered that veterinary visits could be quite costly. She hoped the cost of two back-to-back appointments wasn't going to be too much of a financial strain for Amy.

"Sandy is plenty mad at me for wrangling her into the carrier for her appointments and madder still that I have to give her medication. It's not nearly as easy as the vet said it would be."

"Do you need help giving her the medicine? I'd be happy to help you."

A frown flickered over Amy's face. "No, that's okay. I'm figuring it out."

Sarah barely held in a sigh. It seemed this personal conversation would be coming to an end. It hadn't taken long for Amy to take offense. But Sarah didn't understand why. She was bothered both by her apparent dismay at her offer to help and by her automatic refusal of the offer. Why should the offer seem to make her uncomfortable?

It made Sarah again wonder about Amy's living situation. It seemed that Amy didn't want to have her over at all. Was her living situation really that embarrassing? It must be even less ideal than her own situation of living with college students. Sarah liked her roommates, but living with college students was best done while in college oneself.

Sarah had even considered that maybe Amy's living situation was something unlawful, like living in someone's illegally converted garage. She had read an article in the paper that people sometimes had to do that here because of the high rents in the area. But she didn't get the impression that Amy would do anything illegal. So maybe the problem was that she lived with a girlfriend despite her denial of it. Sarah was torn between asking her for more information or just continuing to enjoy this fling while it lasted. Sarah didn't want to be a party to cheating and someone getting hurt, though. "Look, if you live with someone…"

"I said that I didn't," Amy answered firmly enough that Sarah fully believed her.

"Then I don't understand why we always end up at my house. I don't even know where you live."

"It's complicated."

"Yeah. You said that before."

"Yes, and you said that I didn't have to tell you about it until I was ready."

Sarah sighed. "I tried to tell myself that the details didn't matter since we were only having this fling, but they *do* matter. I don't like secrets." She got up, collected her trash from lunch, and deposited it in a nearby trashcan. She faced her again. "I thought I could do this with you, but I don't know if I can. Let's skip tonight. I think I'll be too tired from the Fun Run, anyway."

"Sarah…"

But Sarah didn't want to wait to hear excuses and kept walking.

* * *

Amy returned to work in her lifeguard tower after lunch at the food truck, feeling dejected despite the bright, beautiful, sunny afternoon. She removed the polo shirt and shorts she had put on over her swimsuit for the lunch break and sat down in her chair to keep watch over the people in her zone. Now that a portion of the beach was no longer closed off for the Fun Run, it was filled with the usual crowds of beachgoers.

Lunch with Sarah had been such a pleasant surprise and had been going well until they had gotten into a personal discussion. Amy knew she shouldn't have answered Sarah's question about what she'd been doing outside of work, knew that it would only lead to trouble. But she had wanted to share more of herself with Sarah. Lunch had seemed almost like a date.

If only Sarah's feelings about wealthy women were clearer, Amy could know how much she could answer. She wouldn't have to deliberate over each question that Sarah asked, deciding how much to reveal and how much not to reveal, and conversation would be so much easier. But she couldn't very well ask. If she did, she would have to explain her reason for asking and reveal too much about herself, possibly causing the very problem that she wanted to avoid.

But she had ended up offending Sarah today anyway. She understood her misgivings about not being invited over. It was nice of her to offer to help give Sandy the medicine and, even if not for that, Amy knew she should have extended an invitation to Sarah to come over by now. Tonight would have been their third time in a row at Sarah's house.

Amy wondered if their time together was over or if their arrangement would resume next week. She wanted very much to see Sarah again and not just because of the sex. Sarah was so interesting, so multifaceted. Who knew she could speak some Vietnamese? Amy found herself wanting to ask Sarah all sorts of questions and find out all of the other fascinating things about her. Unfortunately, it wasn't really her place since they weren't really girlfriends. This fling was making sure of that.

Amy sighed. Between her family and now Sarah, there were a lot of people mad at her. Ever since the trip to the veterinarian, even her cat was mad at her.

The ringing of the tower telephone interrupted her thoughts. She picked up the receiver. It was Communications, calling to warn of the possibility of rip currents developing due to an increasing south swell.

Hanging up the phone, Amy redoubled her efforts to keep watch on the water and the swimmers. Rip currents were strong channels of water flowing from the shore back out to sea. They were characterized by churning, sandy brown water and had three parts: the feeders supplying the water, the fast-moving water of the neck, and the circular area of the head where the water was released out to sea. Rip currents could appear instantly and could easily pull any swimmer out to sea, even strong ones.

Amy didn't see any areas of concern in the ocean in front of her tower, but she did notice one in front of one of the towers flanking hers. The waves there were breaking less cleanly and the water was becoming increasingly foamy. The area was crowded with people playing in the waves and some of them swimming. Upon seeing her neighboring lifeguard, Michael, arrive at the shore to redirect the swimmers to a safer area, she relaxed somewhat.

But it didn't look like all of the swimmers were complying. Or maybe they couldn't because of the current! Two swimmers started waving their hands frantically. Michael entered the water and swam toward them.

Grabbing the phone, Amy notified Communications of the rescue situation and then snatched her rescue can from its hook as she raced out of her tower to help. Communications would contact the patrolling lifeguard boat and the patrolling lifeguard truck to respond with additional help in case it was needed. It would also contact the main tower and the towers flanking her tower and Michael's so that other lifeguards would watch over their areas in their absence.

Reaching the ocean at a sprint, Amy fitted the strap of the rescue can over her head and right shoulder so that it lay across her torso and then high-stepped through the surf, the can trailing behind her on its tether. Diving into the water, she swam diagonally to the area of rip current, thereby avoiding its dangers. Her aim was to arrive at the space between the head and neck. She suspected that the rapidly moving water in the neck was where the swimmers were caught.

Michael reached one of the swimmers and began the process of rescuing him. The other swimmer was still struggling to fight the strong current, panic written on her face. Amy kicked and stroked to get there as fast as she could. The woman's head was sinking lower and lower as the woman frantically splashed about. Arriving, Amy took hold of her rescue can and extended it across the surface of the water toward her. "Grab the handle," Amy shouted over the sound of the sea.

The woman reached for it, gasping and sputtering in the turbulent water but managing to wrap her hands around the grips.

"Good," Amy shouted. "Now try to get your arms across the top of it and let it help support you."

The woman complied, her gasping breaths becoming less frantic with the buoyancy of the rescue can helping her. "The water just kept pulling me," she panted, "and taking me farther out."

"It's a rip current, but it's going to be okay. I'm going to swim us to shore. Can you keep holding onto the can while I do that?"

The woman nodded, calmer now.

"Good," Amy said. The strap of the rescue can still secure around her torso, she started swimming to shore, taking a diagonal path as before and towing the fatigued woman behind her. She stroked hard to navigate the extra weight through the surf and adjusted course as waves broke around them. Reaching the shallower water near shore, she got her footing and helped the woman do the same. Amy guided her out of the water toward dry sand, her arm wrapped around her to lend support.

"The water just kept pulling me," the woman repeated. "I couldn't get back."

"It's okay. You're safe now."

"Thank you. Thank you so much."

"You're welcome. You did the right thing to wave for help. If you get stuck in a current again, you can also try swimming parallel to shore to escape the pull."

Amy guided the woman toward the lifeguard truck and the supervisor that had arrived on scene. First aid needs would be assessed and further help given if needed. Michael and the swimmer he had rescued were also there and it looked like they were okay. Amy was thankful for a successful rescue for everyone. And while there was never a good time for a rip current, the rescue had at least temporarily interrupted her self-recrimination over ruining lunch with Sarah.

CHAPTER NINE

Amy ate a forkful of her serving of the short rib and sweet potato hash that Emilia had prepared for this week's family brunch. The rich, braised meat practically melted in her mouth. She ate another forkful, enjoying the cubes of tender sautéed sweet potato and the savory mixture of onions and seasonings. She sliced off a piece of the fried egg sitting atop her hash and used it to gather up another forkful of the succulent dish.

The topic of conversation was the headlight design on next year's sedan models and Amy only half listened. While she knew that her family was not enthused about her new job, she hadn't expected them to continue ignoring it week after week. Didn't they notice how much happier she was from her job change? Were they not the least bit curious about the job that had inspired her to take a break from her own dealership? A little bit of interest from any of them would be nice.

Maybe it was partly her fault. She had yet to correct their assumption that it was only a summer job. Maybe it was time to break the news to everyone that it wasn't just a seasonal job. Amy waited for a lull in the conversation and cleared her throat. "I want to let all of you know that I've taken a permanent position as a South Coast Beach lifeguard."

Amy saw surprise, confusion, and disapproval around the table. This was precisely why she had been putting off telling everyone. She tried not to squirm as she waited for someone to say something.

"Permanent?" Aurora was the first to speak, and her disbelief was clear.

"Yes, I want to continue being a lifeguard."

"Why?"

"Because being a lifeguard is my passion."

"But you sell cars like the rest of us do."

"Yes, but it's never been a passion for me like it is for all of you." Amy had explained all of this and more to her family months ago when she had decided to take the break from her dealership. She could only hope that they would make more of an effort to understand her choice now that they knew it was not a passing fancy.

"What about your dealership?" her father asked.

"I'm sorry, Dad, but I don't plan to work there any longer. I'll need to sell it."

Her father shook his head. "Just like that? You want to leave a successful business to hang out at the beach?"

Amy drew back. "Is that what you think? That I've made this decision lightly? That I'm doing this to hang out at the beach?"

His silence was telling.

Amy looked around the table at the rest of her family. "Is that what all of you think, that I'm playing in the sand and working on my tan?"

Her family wouldn't meet her gaze.

"If any of you bothered to ask me about my job or learn anything about it, you would know that's not the case. This career change is absolutely not a decision I've made lightly. I can't believe you oppose me in this, even if it is outside the family business." She got up from the table.

"Amy..." her mother said.

"Since I obviously don't have the support of any of you, there's no need to trouble yourselves any longer to fill in at my dealership in my absence. I'm sure that Reynaldo, the finance manager there, will be glad to do it and glad to accept the salary that comes with it." She strode from the room and out of the house.

* * *

Sarah pedaled her bicycle on the bike path that ran along the beach. The afternoon was spectacularly beautiful, the sky a clear blue, the ocean sparkling in the sun, and the sun's rays warm on her body. Moving her legs felt good; it eased the soreness and stiffness from yesterday's Fun Run. She felt foolish for even having bothered to try to impress Amy with her running. Someone so reticent when it came to seemingly benign topics of conversation obviously wasn't truly interested in her.

Maybe it was all just physical for Amy. That was fine, Sarah supposed. That was what they had agreed upon, after all. She just wished she had an easier time continuing to go along with it and enjoying the arrangement for what it was, like Amy seemed to be able to do.

Sarah brought her bike to a stop after reaching Sunrise Beach. A wide stretch of sandy beach like South Coast Beach, it was a popular windsurfing spot. She liked to watch the windsurfers skim over the water on their boards as they harnessed the wind with their sails. She wheeled her bike off the path to an empty bench just outside the parking lot and took a seat.

Ten or so windsurfers were out on the ocean today, each skittering across the water on a board with a different colored sail. Sarah watched them alternately as they maneuvered on and around the waves. Her attention was drawn to the skillful maneuvering of one in particular. He was traveling the length of a breaking wave just as a surfer might be able to do if the conditions were right, only moving much faster due to the wind filling the sail with power. Sarah didn't actually know if the windsurfer was a man but she had yet to see any women out here. He then executed a one hundred and eighty degree turn to seamlessly reverse direction and come back, this time carving the water between swells and throwing a tail of spray into the air with each zig and zag of the board.

Sarah kept her eyes on him as he cut through the water toward a cresting wave. He directed the speeding board up the face of the wave, executing an arcing jump off the top of the wave and into the air. Sarah held her breath, but he landed the jump cleanly and continued clipping along the water at a fast pace. He then turned and began sailing a path to shore, apparently done for the day.

After turning her attention back to the others and watching a few minutes longer, Sarah decided that the best of the show on the water was over. She stood up, taking a moment to shake out her legs that had stiffened again from sitting. Wheeling her bike back to the path, she got on and started to pedal home.

On the portion of the path along the edge of the parking lot, Sarah hit the brakes, coming to an abrupt stop. There, at the end of the parking lot and only a couple cars away, was Amy loading a windsurfing board and gear bag into an SUV.

A fellow cyclist swerved around Sarah. "Hey, watch it!" he called.

"Sorry!" She moved her bike off the path.

Amy looked over, her face registering surprise. "Sarah?"

"Hi!" Sarah smiled. She walked her bike the short distance to her. "Was that you on the water just now? I was over there watching." She gestured in the general direction of the bench where she had been sitting. "You looked amazing, especially doing that jump!"

A grin spread on Amy's face. "Thanks! I was having a blast! The conditions were excellent. I don't think I've ever caught so much air."

Sarah loved hearing the exhilaration in Amy's voice.

"So you're out for a bike ride?"

Sarah nodded. "Yeah. I was just taking a break to watch the action." She eyed Amy's form-fitting wetsuit. "I don't know how I didn't recognize those toned curves of yours when I saw you get out of the water and start walking up the beach. But my vantage point was kind of far." Sarah stepped closer. She reached her hand out and ran it along Amy's shoulder, brushing down over her breast, curving in at her waist, and trailing along her hip. Was Amy naked under that tight material? She brought her gaze up to Amy's lovely agate-colored eyes.

Amy pulled Sarah to her and kissed her. The kiss made Sarah's body sing, and her grip on her bicycle loosened. As her bike started to fall over, she broke the kiss.

Amy helped her catch it. "Here, let's lean that here for a moment." She carefully placed the bike against the shiny SUV.

Sarah did a double take. The SUV was a Lexus. That was unexpected. She looked from the vehicle to Amy. "Is this yours?"

Amy hesitated but then answered. "Yes, it's mine." She sounded resigned, as though she'd been caught at something.

Sarah studied Amy, taking in her guilty expression. She crossed her arms and frowned. "You know, for some reason, I thought you were practically destitute. That first Saturday, it was obvious that you didn't want me to see your car, so I thought it must be an old rattletrap. The second Saturday, you rode a bicycle to my house, so then I wasn't sure that you had a car at all. As it turns out, you have this." She gestured to the expensive vehicle. "Why would you want to hide it?"

Amy hadn't answered, so Sarah continued. "I wonder what else I don't know about you? I'm going to go out on a limb and guess that you live somewhere nice, too. Not the run-down apartment with multiple roommates that you had me imagining with your refusal to tell me where you lived."

When Amy didn't deny it, Sarah knew she had guessed correctly. "Why would you bother with all of these secrets? Is it fun for you to play games?" she asked, spreading her arms wide in a plea.

"What? No, of course not. And I didn't mean to mislead you."

"Then what is it?"

Amy took a breath. "At the coffeehouse, you said that you were drawn to your ex for her wealthy lifestyle. And you also said that you didn't want to date another rich woman. I didn't know what to think, but it seemed like wealth was going to be an issue between us one way or another."

Sarah thought back. She remembered saying those things, but what did that have to do with Amy? Was Amy trying to say that she was wealthy? Was everyone rich in this city, even the lifeguards? Sarah shook her head, not understanding any of it. She looked at her. "Yes, I did say those things at the coffeehouse. But not so fast. I'm don't think all of this is about me. Why not just ask about my time with Robin if you were confused? I want to know the rest of what's going on."

Amy breathed a heavy sigh. "My last name is Bergen. As in Bergen Motors."

"The auto dealerships?"

"Yes. I own one of them."

"So? What does that have to do with anything?" Then it dawned on her. Amy wasn't just a lifeguard; she was a wealthy businesswoman. A lot like Robin was. And like Robin, Amy probably only normally associated with other wealthy people. Sarah glared at Amy. "You think I'm not good enough for you. That's what this is. You didn't want to bring me to your place. I'm a lowly middle school teacher. I'm only good enough to fuck at my place."

"What? No, that's not true at all!" Amy grabbed her hand beseechingly.

"Then what is it?" Sarah asked.

Amy released her hand and started pacing back and forth, apparently gathering her thoughts. She stopped and turned toward Sarah. "It's just that I've learned to be careful. Sometimes money makes girlfriends stay much too long, like you said happened to you with Robin."

Sarah took a breath and considered this. It was a reasonable explanation. But that didn't mean she liked it. She crossed her arms.

Amy continued. "One woman I dated tried to move in, and I don't even think she particularly liked me. But she kept bringing over more and more of her stuff until it seemed like she practically lived with me." Amy sounded exasperated. She ran a hand through her still damp hair. "She even started decorating."

Despite her annoyance, Sarah let out a surprised laugh. She uncrossed her arms.

"It's true." Amy looked at her. "The worst was a hideous pink throw rug that she put on the living room floor. Sandy wouldn't even walk on it."

Sarah laughed again. She didn't think she was going to be able to stay mad at Amy much longer. "Oh, wow. That's too much. Robin should be thankful that I didn't do anything like that."

"I'm glad my U-Haul girlfriend amuses you," Amy said dryly, a tentative smile playing at her lips. "It was really hard to get her to leave me alone."

"I don't doubt it. But why would you think I'm like that? I told you what happened with Robin. I won't be staying with anyone again just because of money."

"Yes, but I had only just met you and I didn't know if you meant it. It's become a habit for me to keep quiet about my background. I'm sorry."

Sarah faced her. "I'm sad you felt the need to hide things from me, but I'll accept your apology because at least it doesn't seem like you were trying to play me for a fool."

"No, never."

"Good. I've had enough of that from one rich woman already." Sarah wished she could forget her time with Robin altogether.

Amy took Sarah's hand in hers, and this time Sarah clasped it. "I wouldn't say that I'm rich, but I am fairly well-off," she said. "I know that you don't want to date another rich woman, but would you consider dating a well-off woman?"

"Hmm," Sarah said, pretending to think about it. "I guess I could try to talk myself into it. But," she paused, giving Amy a smile, "only if this well-off woman kisses like you do."

Amy smiled back. "You mean like this?" She pulled her close and kissed her purposefully.

Breathless after the kiss and more than a little aroused, Sarah leaned back in the circle of Amy's arms. "Yeah. Like that."

Amy grinned.

"But while we're on the subject, I didn't say that I didn't want to date another rich woman."

"No?" Amy asked with a frown.

"No. I distinctly remember saying that I didn't want to date another *stuck-up* rich woman. So you're safe on both counts." Sarah smiled.

Amy smiled back. "I'm glad. Because I really like you." She kissed her again.

"I like you, too," Sarah said. "But I have to say I'm glad I didn't offer to help with your vet bills yesterday like I almost did. I would have seemed like such a fool."

"No, you're sweet to have worried about me." Amy hugged her. "I had no idea that you would think I was broke. I'm sorry I didn't tell you everything sooner. I don't know how I so badly misjudged things."

"It's okay now. It might take another moment for me to wrap my head around all of it, though." Sarah paused. "How *is* your cat, by the way?"

"I'll tell you what—why don't you come over and see for yourself? I'm sure Sandy would like to meet you. And I would love it if you stayed and joined me for dinner."

Sarah tilted her head. "I don't know, it seems like a big step—me seeing where you live."

"Very funny." Amy shook her head and smiled ruefully, obviously knowing that she deserved the teasing. She looked at Sarah expectantly. "How about it? Would you like to come home with me and have dinner?"

"Would this be a date?"

"Yes. Yes, it would be a date."

"No more fling?"

"No more fling."

Sarah smiled. "Then I'd be delighted."

"Great," Amy said with a big smile. "Let me get out of my wetsuit and then get your bike loaded in with my gear and we'll go."

Sarah looked again at the form-fitting material covering Amy's body. "I guess that means you're not naked under there?"

Amy shook her head. "No, I've got a swimsuit on." She started unzipping her wetsuit.

"I guess you do," Sarah said as the swimsuit was revealed. She shrugged. "For now, anyway."

CHAPTER TEN

Amy couldn't help fumbling her keys as she unlocked the door to her condo. Sarah had rested her hand on her thigh for a good portion of the drive home, giving it an occasional squeeze or stroke, her hand getting higher and higher, and it had been a lot to handle. Sarah brought out more intense responses in her body than anyone else ever had. And she was such a kind, wonderful person. Amy hadn't liked hiding things from her, even if it was only during a fling. As enjoyable as the fling had been, she was glad it was over. It was a relief to have Sarah back in her life after almost losing her over misguided secretiveness and it was great to be able to share more of herself with her now and bring her to her home for the first time.

Amy managed to get the door open, the ache Sarah had stoked between her thighs showing no signs of abating. "Come in," she said, smiling at her and resisting the temptation to lead her straight to the bedroom.

"This is a very nice place, Amy." Sarah stood in the living room, taking in the high ceiling, hardwood flooring, gas fireplace, tasteful furnishings, and the abundance of natural lighting from the windows. She walked over to the sliding glass doors that led to the balcony and admired the spectacular view of the ocean. "I see why that girlfriend of yours wanted to move in." She turned back to Amy with a smile.

Amy was still distractingly aroused. In lieu of a reply, she gave her a smile. It must have been a weak smile, because Sarah's face fell in dismay and she put her hands on her hips. "You look awfully uptight over there. You don't think I already want to move in do you?"

"No, no, it's not that." Amy raised her hands in placation. "I'm glad you like the place. I'm just a little, uh, preoccupied. Your touch on the drive here was rather stimulating." She shifted on her feet.

The dismay evaporated from Sarah's face, a corner of her mouth turning up in a knowing smile. "Preoccupied, hmm? Let me see how dire the situation is." She sauntered over to Amy and brazenly cupped her through the thin layer of her swimsuit.

Amy sucked in a breath.

"Hmm, I do detect a certain amount of swelling in the area."

Amy chuckled and put her arms around her. "You make it sound serious."

"Oh, but I can tell that it is serious." Sarah moved her fingers slightly, and Amy sucked in another breath.

"So serious, in fact, that this swimsuit is going to need to come off soon." Sarah slipped a finger of her other hand under one of the straps of the swimsuit and gave it a tug before letting it snap back lightly against Amy's skin.

Amy's center pulsed. "God, Sarah, do you have any idea what you do to me?"

Sarah's eyes moved to Amy's chest, where her nipples had become two hard points pushing against her swimsuit. "I might have some idea," she said, slowly running her palm over one stiff nipple and then the other.

Amy throbbed against the hand still cupping her. "Please, Sarah," she breathed, "you're killing me."

Sarah chuckled. "Well, we can't have that, can we?" She slid the fabric of Amy's swimsuit aside and stroked Amy's wet, swollen length.

"Oh…" Amy moaned.

Sarah smiled and stroked her again. "Is this what you need?"

"Yes," Amy breathed. "I need you, your fingers, your kisses…" With Sarah continuing to stroke her, it was too hard to think. She leaned her head back, enjoying the sensations from Sarah's skillful fingers. Soon she felt her warm mouth on her neck, kissing, licking, gently sucking. Sarah paused at the hollow at the base of Amy's throat, adding a swirl of her tongue.

Amy moaned again. Sarah's fingers felt so good, her warm kisses felt so good. Feeling her climax start to build, she tightened her hold.

With her teeth Sarah lightly grasped one of Amy's stiff nipples through the fabric of the swimsuit and teased it.

"Oh…" Amy said, reveling in the pleasure coursing through her breast.

Sarah moved her mouth to the other nipple, lightly grasping and teasing again, while continuing to stroke her with her fingers.

"Oh yes…" Amy said, feeling her orgasm gather.

Sarah stroked her a little harder and a little faster.

"Yes, yes…" Amy said, tensing with pleasure as the orgasm tore through her.

Sarah softened her movements.

Amy slowly blinked her eyes open and gazed at Sarah.

"See?" Sarah smiled. "I didn't kill you. You're still alive."

"Ha, barely," Amy said, feeling dazed. "I want you, too, but I think I need a moment."

Sarah laughed lightly, clearly pleased with herself. "It's okay. I can wait for a little while. You'd probably planned on having a shower when you got home from windsurfing."

"That's true, but I've got another idea now. Why don't you join me in the shower and then you won't have to wait?"

"Mmm, I like that idea."

Amy grabbed her hand and led her to the shower.

Feeling very sated, Sarah stepped out of Amy's large, stone-tiled shower. She removed one of the plush bath towels from the rack and dried herself and her hair. Amy had left the shower only moments ago to towel off and find a set of clothes for her to borrow. As Sarah was wrapping herself in the soft towel, Amy appeared in the doorway, dressed in drawstring shorts in sweatshirt material and a T-shirt. She held out a pair of similar shorts and a T-shirt for her.

"Are these okay?"

"Sure, but if they're your shorts, I think they're going to be a little snug."

"I don't mind." Amy gave her an easy smile and leaned one shoulder against the doorway, her gaze settling on the curve of her buttocks in the towel.

Sarah laughed. "You're incorrigible." She put a hand on Amy's chest and gently pushed her from the doorway. "Now go, so I can get dressed."

Amy raised her hands innocently. "All right, I'm going." She backed from the bathroom into the bedroom. "Feel free to borrow whatever else you need—comb, brush, toiletries…" she called as she left.

Warmed by Amy's thoughtfulness and the ease of not having to ask to borrow things, Sarah opened drawers until she found a wide-toothed comb. After combing her damp hair back from her face, she dressed and left the bathroom. She was tempted to pause in Amy's bedroom to learn more about her but didn't want to violate her trust now that she had finally invited her over. She walked into the kitchen where she was pulling food from the large stainless-steel refrigerator and setting it on the granite countertop.

Amy stopped what she was doing and gave her a smile. "You make my plain T-shirt and sweat shorts look very cute."

Sarah felt herself blush. It was a simple compliment, but it was nice to hear.

"Very cute, indeed," Amy said, moving closer. She put her arms around Sarah and gave her a lingering kiss. "I'm already starting to want you again. You have quite an effect on me, Ms.—" Amy tilted her head at Sarah.

"Wagner," Sarah supplied, trying not to think about how impersonal things had been with the fling that they hadn't learned each other's last names until today.

"Wagner," Amy echoed. She kissed her again and dropped her hands to Sarah's buttocks.

"And you have quite an effect on me, Ms. Bergen," Sarah said. Amy's kisses and the warm grasp of her hands on her buttocks had already made her wet again. "So if I'm to be a good dinner guest tonight, we better stop now."

Amy chuckled and released her. She surveyed the food that she had been setting on the counter, as if pretending to see it for the first time. "That's right. I was doing something here before you came into the kitchen to distract me."

Sarah laughed. "What are you making?"

"Fish tacos. Is that all right?"

"Yum! I love fish tacos."

"Good, me too."

"I should mention that I'd never even heard of them until I moved to southern California. Now I can't get enough."

"Oh? Where are you from originally?"

"Iowa."

"And what brought you out here?"

Sarah gestured toward the ocean visible through the window. "All of this beautiful coastline and good weather, for starters. Some of the things that bring everyone here, I imagine. I also wanted to be somewhere where I could more easily be openly gay."

Amy nodded. "Yeah, that's important for me, too. Unfortunately, not everyone is tolerant here, either."

"Yeah, I know," Sarah said. "But at least so far when I've walked with a girlfriend, no one has tried to swerve off the road to run us over."

"What?" Amy exclaimed. "Someone did that to you?"

"Yeah, when I was in college. Two guys in a truck. They were yelling all sorts of things while they were driving, and so, luckily, we heard them in time to jump out of the way. It was scary, though."

"I'll bet." Amy reached for Sarah, enveloping her in a comforting hug against her solid body.

"Yes, and it could have been worse. Maybe it's better there now, I don't know, but I was only too happy to leave as soon as I finished college."

Amy smoothed her hand over Sarah's hair and pressed a kiss to her head as Sarah snuggled against her. "I, for one, am glad you chose to make your way to South Coast Beach."

"I am, too," Sarah said softly. After allowing herself another a moment to enjoy the embrace, she straightened. "Now, what can I do to help with dinner?"

"Well, let's see…" Amy described plans for the ingredients that she had set out. They divided up the tasks and worked together to prepare dinner.

"Here, taste this and tell me what you think." Amy held out a spoonful of the pico de gallo salsa she had just finished making.

Sarah paused in her slicing and cubing of the cantaloupe they were to have for dessert and opened her mouth for the salsa sample. As she chewed, she considered the balance of tastes. "It's good. Those are flavorful tomatoes. And the right amount of onions. But maybe it needs a little bit more cilantro?"

"I think you're right about more cilantro. Maybe a bit more salt, too." She made the adjustments and gave her another taste.

"Mmm, really good now."

Amy set the bowl of salsa next to the dish of Cotija cheese that she had crumbled and the bowl of cabbage that Sarah had finely shredded. "Let me warm the tortillas and broil the fish, and we'll be ready to eat."

"Okay," Sarah said. She was thoroughly enjoying herself sharing these simple activities with the newly open and personable Amy. Was it really going to be this comfortable and easy to move from the fling to dating? She wanted to think so. She finished cutting the melon into bite-size chunks and put it in the refrigerator to chill.

Amy wrapped the tortillas in foil and put them in the oven. As she began cutting the fish into chunks and arranging it on a broiler pan, a cat meowed.

"Sandy! There you are," Amy said. She turned to Sarah. "That's my cat, Sandy. She knows it's dinner time." She put the fish in the oven and washed her hands. "I'm afraid that I have a bad habit of supplementing her cat food with treats from the table. I can't help but think it gets boring to eat just kibble or a can of food each day."

Sarah nodded. "Yeah, it's hard to resist spoiling pets." She approached Sandy and held out her hand. "Hi, Sandy."

Sandy gave her a brief sniff and then butted her hand with her head, asking to be petted. Sarah smiled. She gave Sandy a good petting, and the cat flopped onto the floor, purring.

"This is good for Sandy. She can use a friendly face, I'm sure," Amy said as she watched. "She's tired of me giving her the medication. And unfortunately, she's due for a pill right about now."

"Poor kitty. Taking pills is no fun." Sarah knelt and petted her some more. She glanced over at Amy. "I'd still be happy to help you give her a pill if you like."

"That's kind of you. You were kind to offer yesterday, too. I wish I had accepted then. I'm sorry for being an ass."

"It's okay. You had your reasons," Sarah said.

"For being an ass?" Amy asked with a laugh.

"Yes," Sarah said, smiling back.

Amy shook her head. "You make me forget all of those reasons so easily."

"I'm glad." Sarah held her gaze for a moment and then resumed petting Sandy. "Sandy seems very relaxed. Do you want to go get a pill for her?"

"Actually, the fish will be done soon," Amy said, eyeing the oven. "We better wait until after dinner."

"Why? Giving her a pill will only take a moment."

"A moment?" Amy sounded surprised. "Not after she spits out the pill a few times and I have to pry her mouth open to put it back in each time before she finally swallows it."

"Wow, you *have* been having a tough time." Sarah shook her head. "I had a cat who had to take a course of medicine once, too, and I got pretty good at giving her pills. Would you like me to try with Sandy?"

"I'd be glad to watch and learn if you're willing to show me, but I'm afraid that she might try to scratch you."

Sarah petted Sandy again. "I think I'll be okay, but you can help me by holding her."

"Okay." Amy sounded doubtful, but she got one of Sandy's pills and handed it to Sarah before joining her on the floor with Sandy. Amy petted Sandy and then moved to hold her for Sarah.

"All right, here goes." Sarah gently clasped Sandy's head with her left hand and tilted it back, causing her mouth to open slightly. Holding the pill between the thumb and forefinger of her right hand, she used her middle finger to gently open Sandy's mouth the rest of the way and then quickly dropped the pill behind the base of her tongue. She released her jaw and gently rubbed her throat to encourage her to swallow the pill while murmuring soothing words to her.

"Wow, I think she swallowed it already." Amy looked at Sarah with an expression of wonder.

Sarah smiled. "Yes, I think she did." She petted Sandy once more. "You're a good kitty, Sandy." She stood up.

"For this dose, anyway," Amy said, shaking her head. She released Sandy and stood up, too.

Sandy walked away, giving them a reproachful look over her shoulder for their trickery.

"Thank you for doing that." Amy gave Sarah a squeeze on the arm. "The whole thing went a lot more smoothly tonight, so I'm sure Sandy appreciates it as much as I do. I'll be trying your technique tomorrow."

"Glad to help," Sarah said.

"Now, I better get our fish out of the oven." The fish sizzling under the broiler in the oven had filled the condo with hunger-inducing aromas. Amy walked into the kitchen and washed her hands. Putting on oven mitts, she retrieved the broiler pan full of chunks of flaky white fish and the foil packet of tortillas.

"Mmm, looks perfect," Sarah said. She went over to the sink and washed her hands.

Sandy meowed and approached the kitchen again.

Amy looked at her cat and chuckled. "I'll tell you what, Sandy. You can have the first piece of fish since you took your pill so nicely tonight." She flaked a chunk of fish into small pieces and checked for bones before putting the pieces in a dish. The pieces had already cooled enough for Sandy to eat, so she set the dish down next to her bowl of kibble. "Here you go."

Sandy dug in.

"Must be as good as it looks and smells," Sarah said.

"Yes, so let's make our tacos." Amy handed Sarah a plate and gestured to the array of food. "Go ahead."

"Thanks." Sarah placed a couple of warm corn tortillas on her plate. Then, she placed a piece of fish in the center of each, topping each with the crisp, finely shredded cabbage, the fresh salsa, and the crumbled Cotija cheese.

Amy followed behind her and assembled a few tacos of her own. "Would you like to eat outside on the balcony?"

"I'd love to." Sarah walked over to the sliding glass door with her plate.

"Oh, and we need something to drink," Amy said. She set her plate down. "What would you like? I haven't even offered you anything yet. What kind of hostess am I?"

Sarah smiled and retraced her steps to stand in front of her. "The kind that gives me a double orgasm in the shower before dinner." She planted a kiss on her lips.

A slow, self-sure grin appeared on Amy's face. "Yeah, I guess we've been kind of busy."

"Very," Sarah said. "To answer your question, I'd like a glass of white wine if you have it. If not, water is fine." She picked up Amy's dinner plate with her free hand. "I can take our food outside while you get our drinks."

A moment later, after Sarah had seated herself at the balcony table in the warm summer evening sun, Amy stepped onto the balcony with two glasses of wine. "I hope you like sauvignon blanc." She set a glass before each of their plates and joined her at the table.

"I do," Sarah said. She picked up her glass. "Let's toast."

Amy held up her glass. "What would you like to toast?"

"Here's to a wonderful first date."

Amy clinked her glass to hers. "I couldn't agree more."

They sipped their wine and then began to eat. As Sarah enjoyed the citrus and herbal flavors in the wine, she couldn't help thinking of the way Justin equated wine with relationships. How would the characteristics of sauvignon blanc fit into the scheme of dating? Whichever way it did, it must be good, because not much was better than having a delicious dinner with an ocean view and a beautiful woman, especially a woman who was turning out to be much more pleasant now that she had let her walls down. Sarah was so glad to be able to ask personal questions now.

"What made you decide to become a lifeguard?"

Amy finished eating a bite of taco before replying. "Basically, it was something I thought about pursuing when I was younger but didn't happen until just this year."

"Really? I kind of thought you'd been a lifeguard forever. You look so poised on the deck of your tower, like you're confident that you can handle any problem that comes along."

Amy smiled. "That's really nice to hear. A lot about being a lifeguard feels like second nature to me. I did the junior lifeguard program every year when I was younger, and it became a part of me. But then things got a little complicated."

Between bites of food and sips of wine, Amy explained about her history with Peter, going away to college with a swimming scholarship, and letting herself get swept up in the family business.

Sarah listened attentively, enjoying learning more about Amy.

"One day last year, stuck in traffic yet again on my hour-long commute to my dealership in Santa Ana in order to spend my day doing something I can't seem to enjoy like the rest of my family does, I decided that I needed to make a change. So, I got myself in shape to do the lifeguard tryouts earlier this year and was fortunate enough to get hired. Now I get to do a job that I enjoy."

"I think that's really great," Sarah said.

"Thanks. Me too. I'm much happier now." Amy paused. "My family is less than thrilled with my job change, though."

"Are they afraid for you? Afraid that you might have to risk your life?"

"If they are, they haven't mentioned it. I don't think they take my new job seriously."

"Oh."

"Yeah. We argued about it earlier today, as a matter of fact. I told them that I want to sell my dealership. The idea that I would leave the family business is difficult for them to understand."

"That's too bad. I'm sure you could use their support."

"Yeah." Amy sighed. "And that's not the only stressful thing about this. Another problem is that I need to find a buyer in the next several months if I'm to keep my job as a lifeguard."

"Why is that?"

"I'm still paying off the loan for my dealership. To meet the terms of the loan, I rely not only on profits but also on my general manager salary."

"Do that mean you'll have to return to working at your dealership if you don't find a buyer soon?"

"Yes." Amy ran her hand through her hair and looked away. "I guess I didn't plan my job change very well. But when the opportunity of lifeguard tryouts came along, I had to seize it."

"It sounds like you did what you needed to do." Sarah reached for her hand and gave it a squeeze. "I wish I could help."

Amy smiled and returned her squeeze. "You are helping. Just by listening and understanding my choice. I appreciate it."

Sarah smiled and sipped the last of her wine.

"Would you like another glass?" Amy asked.

Sarah shook her head. "No, thanks. I'm a bit of a lightweight where drinking is concerned. Any more than a glass will give me trouble sleeping."

"Me too, actually. I'll go get us some water and get our dessert." She stood and picked up their empty glasses.

"I'll help." She collected their empty plates.

A few moments later, they returned to their seats at the balcony table, each with a dessert dish of the cubed cantaloupe and a glass of water. The sun had dipped low on the horizon over the ocean, and the air was a little cooler. A small shiver ran through Sarah.

"Are you cold? Should we go inside?" Amy asked.

Sarah shook her head. "No, the evening is too nice. I'll be okay while we finish eating." She picked up her fork.

"All right, but let me at least get you a sweatshirt. I think I might need one, too. Just a sec, I'll be right back." Amy went into the condo. She returned, handing a sweatshirt to Sarah and putting one on herself before sitting back down.

Sarah put the sweatshirt on and immediately felt warmer. The one Amy had put on looked familiar. "Isn't that—"

"Your sweatshirt that I'm wearing? Yeah," She answered with a smile. It was the sweatshirt Sarah had lent her after their first night together. "I can't part with it just yet. It smells too good. Like you." She gazed at her.

"Is that so?" Sarah asked softly, holding her gaze.

"Yes. Even if the fragrance on it is fainter now."

"Hmm, we should do something to fix that problem for you," Sarah said, tapping a finger to her chin as if in deep thought. "I could try sitting a lot closer to you and see if that would help."

"Okay." Amy scooted her chair over a little to make room on her side of the table.

"Actually, I had something else in mind." She arose from her chair and walked the couple of steps to her. She trailed one hand across Amy's shoulders and then draped her arm around her as she lowered herself to sit sideways across her lap, pressing close to her. "Do you think this will help?"

"It will help something, all right." Amy encircled her with her arms and nuzzled her neck.

Sarah slid her fingers into Amy's soft hair and around to the back of her neck, enjoying the sensation of her warm lips on her throat. "Oh, but wait a moment," Sarah said.

"Hmm?" Amy asked distractedly as she paused and looked up at her.

"Let's not forget about dessert, now," Sarah said. With the fingers of one hand, she reached for a piece of cantaloupe from Amy's dish and held it up. "You don't mind if we share, do you?" A drop of juice fell to her wrist. She licked it.

Amy went still, watching. "Um, what? Uh, no, go right ahead."

Another drop of juice fell, and Sarah licked that one too. Then she slowly opened her mouth and placed the cube of melon inside, ending with a suggestive flourish of her tongue and lips on her finger.

Amy's eyes darkened.

"Mmm, this is good melon." Sarah sighed in pleasure while she chewed.

Amy's lips parted.

"Oh, that's right—we were going to share." Picking up another cube of melon, she brought it toward Amy's parted lips. Slowly, she rubbed the juicy cube of melon across the surface of her bottom lip. Taking the melon away, she traced the same path with her tongue, licking and sucking the juice from Amy's lip.

Amy moaned, tightening her arms around her and returning the kiss. After a nice, long kiss, she broke away to look at her. "Do you mind if we take the rest of dessert inside?"

Sarah leaned back in the circle of her arms and smiled. "Not at all." She took the dish of melon and stood up. "Because I'd love to undress you and then eat a few more of these pieces off your body."

"Oh, my God," Amy said, sprawling dramatically in the chair.

Sarah laughed and walked over to the sliding glass door, opening it. "Don't you want to come?" she asked, arching an eyebrow as she waited.

"You have no idea how much," Amy said, quickly standing.

"Oh, I think I do," Sarah said and walked into the condo with Amy right behind her.

CHAPTER ELEVEN

Sarah poured herself a large mug of coffee from the carafe in the teachers' lounge.

"What are you doing? That stuff is deadly!" Justin exclaimed.

"I know," Sarah said, stifling a yawn, "but I was too tired to make my own this morning." She slid into a chair across from him at the table and took a large sip of the coffee. "I had a bit of a late night last night." She felt her lips spread into a smile at the memory of dessert with Amy.

"The good kind of late night from the looks of it," he said. "Do tell."

"It *was* a good night—I was at Amy's place."

Justin's jaw dropped. "You finally went to her place? She let you see it?"

"Mm-hm." Sarah took another sip of coffee to draw out the suspense.

"Come on, tell me," he said. "Was it as bad as you thought? Did you walk in, take one look, and say, 'What a dump'?" he said in an excellent Bette Davis imitation.

Sarah laughed. "I wouldn't do that."

"Oh, you know I'm just teasing." He touched her arm. "But really, what was it like?"

"It's a beachfront condo."

"What!"

"It's true," Sarah said with a nod.

"How does a lifeguard have a beachfront condo?"

"I'll tell you how, because I found out something else from her yesterday, too—her last name is Bergen."

"Bergen," Justin repeated. He squinted at her. "Bergen. As in Bergen Motors?"

Sarah nodded and drank more coffee.

"Ah, that explains the condo." He paused. "But if she's a Bergen, what's she doing as a lifeguard?"

"It's complicated," Sarah answered. She chuckled to herself when she realized that she sounded like Amy. "Basically, she tried the family auto business but doesn't like it. Being a lifeguard is her childhood dream, so she went for it this year and is trying to sell her dealership."

"Huh," Justin said. "Well, good for her."

"Yeah, I think so, too."

"Why didn't she tell you about herself sooner?"

"I guess she's had some clingy girlfriends, so she keeps quiet about things until she knows someone better."

"Oh," Justin said. "Is that the only reason?"

"And she was wary of me because of my time with Robin."

"Oh," he said again. "I can see how that might have concerned her."

"Yeah, so I can't be too mad over it, even though I'd told her I'd learned from my mistakes with Robin."

"Well, what about you with her? Is she another Robin?"

"No. She's nothing like Robin, thank goodness."

"That's good. I'm happy for you then."

"Me, too. I had a great time with her yesterday. The fling was fun, but dating and getting to know one another feels a lot better to me."

"But...if she's going to keep secrets like that, aren't you worried that she might do it again?"

Sarah frowned. "I hadn't thought about it. What kind of secrets?"

"I don't know—that's why they're called secrets."

Sarah shook her head. "Not helping."

"Sorry, I was just saying..."

She sipped her coffee. "That's okay. I know you're only watching out for me."

He nodded.

"I don't think there's anything to worry about, but I'll be careful." Careful, but not suspicious. Sarah wasn't going to go looking for problems. "So what did you and Ron do this weekend?"

Justin smiled. "We had a great time, too. We drove up to West Hollywood for brunch yesterday and then went to a revival house showing a double feature of *Into the Forest* and *Dead Ringer*."

"Ah, that explains why your Bette Davis imitation was even more spot-on than usual."

He grinned.

She drained the last of her coffee and stood up. "Going to the movies sounds fun. I haven't been in a while."

He stood up, too. "You could always go to one with your new girlfriend."

"You're right, I could. Because I do have a girlfriend now, not just a fling. I wonder what kind of movies she likes."

"I don't know, but we better get headed to our classrooms. And just think, only two more weeks until school is out."

Sarah smiled at the thought of summer break and more time with Amy.

CHAPTER TWELVE

Amy stood in her walk-in closet in dress slacks and a bra. She couldn't decide which shirt to wear for tonight's date with Sarah. Already having put on and taken off one shirt, she was now flipping through the others hanging on the rack. Today, the Friday of this first week of June, Sarah's school had let out, and Amy was taking her to a nice restaurant to celebrate the start of her summer vacation. The restaurant was near the beach and only a couple of blocks from the pier, but it served food that was far nicer than the usual beach fare that most of the restaurants there served and Amy was dressing for the occasion.

Since their impromptu dinner date at the condo, they had gone out to eat at a couple small cafés. The dates at the cafés had been fun. She and Sarah had each taken the other to their favorite place for fish tacos and then seen a movie. While both cafés served good fish tacos, it was agreed that the ones at the condo had been the best. As for the movies, the first had been a romantic comedy that had been pretty entertaining. The second had been a thriller with too many special effects, but the lead actress had been hot, so they had both enjoyed it anyway.

This would be their first date in a more formal setting and somehow it seemed more important. Maybe that's why it was making her a little nervous. Going on dates for tacos and movies didn't require wearing anything dressy, so she had yet to wear anything other than shorts and casual shirts around Sarah. She wanted to take extra care to look nice for her tonight. She reached for another shirt, put it on, and stepped out of the closet to inspect herself in the mirror. Like the first shirt, it didn't quite work. She took it off and discarded it next to the other.

She was running out of time. Maybe a sweater would be the thing to wear. She walked over to her dresser and opened the drawer where she kept her summer-weight sweaters. Choosing one, she pulled it on. She checked her reflection in the mirror and debated whether to try on a different one. But she needed to leave. She grabbed her keys and wallet, petted Sandy goodbye, and headed out.

When a knock sounded at the door, Sarah eagerly got up to answer it. Amy was right on time to pick her up for their date. She cut a dashing figure in dark slacks and what looked to be a designer sweater. The sweater's lightweight fabric clung to every curve of her strong and supple torso and its bold stripes of alternating navy blue and navy heather served to highlight her athletic shoulders, full bust, and trim waist. Three-quarter sleeves that Amy had pushed up even further revealed a tantalizing portion of her toned arms. It was a good thing that Sarah's roommates were home for once, or she might not have been able to resist the temptation to pull Amy into the house and make them more than a little late for tonight's reservation. Sarah settled for greeting her with a kiss; there would be plenty of time for more later.

"You look amazing in that sweater."

"Thanks, you look amazing yourself," Amy said, her eyes sweeping over Sarah. Sarah was gratified by the compliment because she had sifted through dress after dress in her closet tonight before selecting this shift dress patterned in shades of blue. She wanted to look good for Amy on their first date in a nice restaurant and knew that the back darts on this dress made it snug in at her waist to flatter her figure and that its split neckline allowed a tasteful glimpse of cleavage.

Amy drove them to the restaurant and pulled up in the drive. A valet immediately stepped forward to open the door for Sarah and another hurried over to do the same for Amy. If valet service was this attentive here, it must be a very nice restaurant. Sarah stepped out of the SUV with a smile of thanks to the valet and moved to the sidewalk to wait for Amy. Amy handed off her keys to the other valet and, arriving at her side, placed a hand at the small of her back and escorted her up the walkway to the restaurant.

The interior was lovely, with cream-colored walls above wooden wainscoting. Wide, bowl-shaped pendant lights hung from the recessed ceiling and cast a soft glow on the tablecloth-covered tables and upholstered chairs. Picture windows that were partially covered by sun shades in a muted color supplied a view of the beach and ocean. It was wonderful, and even more wonderful to be here with Amy.

The hostess guided them to their table and left them with menus, a wine list, and a list of specialty cocktails.

Sarah perused the list of cocktails. It was varied, and many of the drinks listed contained herbs, house-made syrups, and other fresh ingredients. "These all sound good. I think I'm going to try one." She looked across the table at Amy. "That is, unless you'd like to order a bottle of wine."

"No, go right ahead. You know me—I'm probably just going to order some mineral water. But I'd love a taste of whichever cocktail you choose, if that's all right."

"Sure. You know how much I enjoy sharing with you." She held Amy's gaze and gave her a wink and was rewarded when Amy blushed. She felt her own face heat at the memory of sharing the cantaloupe that other night, of trailing a piece of the fruit over Amy's breasts and around her nipples and licking the juice from her skin, and then repeating the process as she got lower and lower until she was exactly where she wanted to be. And then experiencing Amy doing the same to her.

A corner of Amy's mouth twitched into a smile. She clearly knew what Sarah was thinking.

Their waiter appeared tableside. "Good evening. What can I get you to drink tonight?"

Sarah cleared her throat. "The raspberry vodka gimlet, please."

"And for you?" The waiter looked to Amy.

"Mineral water," she answered. The blush in her cheeks and hint of a smile lingered. She looked beautiful.

The waiter recited the night's specials before departing. Amy picked up her menu to consider the rest of the choices, as did Sarah.

"Since we didn't come here for fish tacos," Sarah said, "I was planning to branch out and order something other than fish, but the wood oven-roasted halibut with Meyer lemon buerre blanc sounds too good to pass up."

Amy nodded. "I was thinking the same thing about the wild king salmon with summer chanterelles. Maybe I'll go all in and order a seafood appetizer as well, because the crab-stuffed squash blossoms sound delicious." She set her menu aside.

"They do. Can I try a bite?"

"Sure. You know how much I enjoy sharing with you, too." Amy held Sarah's gaze and gave her a teasing smile.

Sarah smiled and shook her head. Amy chuckled.

The waiter placed Sarah's drink before her and opened Amy's bottle of mineral water, pouring it into a glass for her. After taking their food orders, he departed.

Amy raised her glass. "To the start of your summer vacation."

Sarah smiled and touched her glass to Amy's. "Thank you. And thank you for taking me out to celebrate."

"You're welcome." Amy sipped her mineral water.

Sarah took a sip of her cocktail. The sweetness of the muddled raspberries and sugar was tempered by the zing of fresh lime juice, and the drink had just the right amount of vodka. "It's good," she announced, passing it to her.

Amy took a sip. "It is." She passed it back.

Sarah took another sip. "It's too bad there's no summer vacation for you."

"Yeah, summer is our busy season. In fact, it got under way last weekend—Memorial Day. But the best part about summer is that the junior lifeguard program starts soon."

"In a couple of weeks, right?"

"Yes, for everyone who made it at the tryouts."

"You must be excited."

"I am. I'm looking forward to meeting the kids and teaching them new skills. It's going to be great watching them gain confidence and rise to the challenges we put before them while they have fun doing it."

"What kinds of things do they get to do each day?"

"Each day there are workouts, lessons, games, and events. The workouts are things like running, swimming, kayaking, paddleboarding, and calisthenics. The lessons mostly revolve around basic lifeguarding skills, such as the common types of injuries and problems we see and the rescue techniques and first aid techniques we use for each one. Other lessons are on subjects like nutrition, sun protection, and sportsmanship."

Sarah nodded. It sounded like a fun, challenging, and educational program.

"But it's summer, so the program is not all workouts and studying. The kids get to bodyboard and surf or learn how if they don't know, play beach volleyball, have relay races, and do a lot of other fun stuff like go on field trips to places like tide pools and an aquarium so they can see marine life up close."

"And don't forget the pier jump," Sarah said. "I know all about that from Hannah, Mandy, and some of my other students who can't wait to do it."

Amy laughed. "That's right, and there's also a pier swim, where they swim around the pier."

The waiter arrived and placed the appetizer of crab-stuffed squash blossoms on the table.

Sarah admired the attractively arrayed dish. There were two squash blossoms nestled together on an artistic smear of green sauce—tomatillo, if Sarah recalled correctly from the menu. The orange-yellow blossoms had been stuffed to a nice plumpness and had been so delicately fried that the filling was still entirely contained within each closed blossom.

"Would you like one?" Amy asked.

Sarah nodded, picking up her fork. Reluctant to ruin the creation, she delicately pressed the side of her fork onto the stuffed blossom to cut off a bite containing the flower and the filling. She put the bite in her mouth. Closing her eyes for a moment while she chewed, she savored the flavors of the sweet crab meat and the blend of melted cheeses.

Amy smiled. "Good, huh?"

Sarah nodded and took another bite.

Amy reached for her own fork and began making equally quick work of the other blossom.

"So, the pier swim…" Sarah said. "That must be far. The South Coast Beach pier is pretty big."

"Yes, swimming out and back means swimming a little over two-thirds of a mile through the waves. But the kids can do it. We have them nice and fit by the end of the summer."

"It sounds like it. And from what I saw at the tryouts, a lot of them are good swimmers to begin with."

"That they are."

A busboy removed the empty plate and forks.

"Do you want kids of your own?" Sarah asked. She regretted her question as soon as it left her mouth. "I'm sorry. I guess it's a little early to ask that." She tittered nervously.

"No, it's okay." Amy reached for her hand across the table. She covered it with her other hand and gave it a reassuring pat. "It's not too early to ask." She took a breath and appeared to be carefully considering her answer.

Sarah couldn't blame her. It was a loaded question. She still felt bad for asking it, but all the talk about the kids in the junior lifeguard program had made her curious and she liked Amy well enough to want to know her thoughts on the subject. But now that she had asked the question, she was kind of afraid to know the answer. What if Amy's reply wasn't going to be something she liked? Things could sour between them very quickly and Sarah didn't want that.

"No, I don't want kids," Amy said. There was tension in her hand as it held hers. She must be similarly concerned about the implications of her answer. Sarah warmed at the thought that Amy might care enough about her for that to be the case. Amy squinted at Sarah as though to brace herself for her coming response. "Is not wanting kids a deal breaker?"

Sarah squeezed her hand reassuringly. "No, it's not a deal breaker at all. Quite the opposite. I don't want kids, either."

Amy leaned back with obvious relief. "Whew, for a minute I thought this celebration dinner was going to come to a quick end."

"Sorry for that," Sarah said with a grimace. "I'll try not to ask any more momentous questions tonight if I can help it."

Amy gave a small chuckle. "Okay, but while we're on the subject, why don't you want kids?"

"I suppose it does seem a little odd, considering that I'm a middle school teacher."

"No," Amy said. "No more odd than me being a junior lifeguard instructor and not wanting them."

Sarah nodded. "Kids are great and I like teaching them and being around them, but I also like leaving them at the end of the day."

"Me, too." Amy smiled at her.

She smiled back. It was heartening to know that they were on the same page on a topic that probably would have come up sooner rather than later the way their relationship seemed to be progressing.

The waiter reappeared and placed their main courses before them.

"Mmm, these look as delicious as the appetizer," Amy said. "And they smell wonderful."

They ate dinner, discussing and sharing their food and other topics of conversation. After their empty plates had been removed, the waiter brought dessert menus before departing again.

"What do you think?" Amy looked at Sarah.

"I'm pretty full, but everything has been so good that I think I want to try dessert, too. I'll just get something light."

"No one will have to twist my arm to convince me to try dessert, either."

The waiter returned and took their orders. They both declined his suggestion of coffee with their desserts. He soon returned with a scoop of the seasonal sorbet for Sarah and the bittersweet chocolate pot de crème for Amy.

Sarah took a spoonful of the sorbet placed before her. "Mmm." The dessert melted against her tongue, filling her mouth with an icy silkiness and the heady flavor of fresh peaches. "You've got to try this." She pushed her dish toward the center of the table to share.

"Mmm, same here," Amy said, pushing her own dish toward Sarah.

Sarah took a spoonful of it. The thick and rich chocolate custard coated her tongue. "Oh, this is good too."

"Yours too," Amy said, having tried a spoonful of the sorbet.

They continued sharing the desserts until they had scraped the last bits from each of the dishes. The waiter deposited the bill on the table and Amy paid it.

"Thank you for this lovely dinner. It was wonderful," Sarah said.

"You're welcome. I'm glad you enjoyed it. It was wonderful for me, too."

Walking out of the restaurant, they emerged into the night air.

"It's nice out," Sarah said. "Still warm."

"Yes, the marine layer hasn't settled in yet."

"I love these late evening summer sunsets." The long South Coast Beach pier stood out in relief against the backdrop of a multihued sunset, illuminated by the light standards that lined either side of it.

"Would you like to go for a walk on the pier for a closer look?" Amy asked.

"I would love to walk on the pier with you at sunset." Sarah took Amy's hand.

Amy waved away the valet, and they began walking the couple of blocks to the pier. With the summer season and the balmy evening, the area was busy. Shops were open even at this late hour and still doing a brisk business, and the restaurants were crowded.

They turned onto the pier. Paved with concrete, it afforded easy walking. Sarah strolled alongside Amy in her dressy sandals with no fear of tripping on a gap between timber ties or of getting splinters. Nearby other couples strolled hand in hand and a woman pushed a toddler in a stroller, holding her cell phone to her ear while a second child ran excitedly about, looking at the waves through the railings on either side of the pier. A tourist couple paused to snap a picture of the gorgeous sunset.

"Why don't we stop for a moment, too," Amy said.

"Okay," Sarah said. Having walked about two-thirds of the way onto the pier, they were well over the water with an excellent view of the waves and the sunset. She walked to one side of the pier to stand at the railing.

Amy stopped next to her, placing her arm around her, and Sarah leaned into her embrace. She looked to the horizon, which was colored a breathtaking blend of red, orange, and yellow by the last rays of the sun. "Beautiful, isn't it?" Amy remarked.

Sarah turned her gaze from the horizon to her. The fading light caught the planes and curves of Amy's face, making her tan skin golden and her agate-colored eyes mesmerizing. "Very beautiful," Sarah said.

Amy smiled and then, leaning closer, kissed her.

A momentary breeze made Sarah give a slight shiver in her sleeveless dress.

"Getting cold?" Amy asked. She moved behind her and encircled her with her arms.

"Mmm, better." Sarah leaned back into Amy's warm body, enjoying the comfort and protection of her embrace while watching the last of the sunset. "This is nice." She sighed in contentment.

"It is." Amy pressed a kiss to Sarah's hair.

A cry of "Brandon! Get down from there!" shattered the tranquility.

Sarah straightened and turned to the source of the cry, as did Amy. It seemed to have come from the woman who had been walking with the young boy and pushing the stroller. She was on the other side of the pier, about forty feet away, holding her phone in one hand while reaching for the boy with the other. He was astride the pier railing.

Amy took off, running toward them.

Sarah followed as quickly as she could, running in her sandals. The woman must have been sitting on the nearby bench while on the phone and not noticed the boy climb onto the railing. The other child fortunately still looked to be in the stroller, which was visible in the light cast by an overhead lamp post.

Sarah watched in alarm as the boy obstinately shrugged away from his mother's reach and climbed down the ocean side of the railing. He inched along the limited space, gripping the railing with only one hand and extending the other for balance. His mother grabbed for him, and he took his hand from the railing to avoid her reach. Losing his balance, he pinwheeled his arms and fell backward off the pier. Sarah gasped in horror.

"Brandon!" His mother let out a terrified scream. She extended her arm over the railing as if to somehow reach him before he fell into the sea below. "Brandon!" she cried again.

Amy skidded to a stop at the railing and peered over the side where the boy fell in. Immediately, she stepped back and began tugging off her shoes and socks.

Reaching her side, Sarah also looked over the railing into the area of surf where the boy had gone in, straining to see in the ebbing light. The sea was quite dark now and she didn't see him. She looked at Amy.

"Call 911! I'm going in, but we might need help." Amy was peeling off her clothes, stripping down to her bra and underwear, clearly not wanting the burden of her sweater and pants in the cold, dark water when she went after the boy.

Sarah fumbled in her purse for her phone and, with trembling fingers, dialed the emergency number. Waiting for the call to connect, she peered over the railing again. She caught a glimpse of something in the dimly lit water. Was that him? Was he moving on his own, or were the waves just tossing him about? The emergency operator came on the line and Sarah began speaking.

A crowd was gathering with the commotion. People pushed closer as they tried to see what was happening.

The woman turned around with a frantic look in her eyes. "Somebody help me! My boy is down there!"

Amy's state of partial undress must have registered with the distraught mother, because a flash of relief crossed over her face. "Are you going to get him? Hurry! Please hurry!"

Amy was already climbing over the railing to the other side. Once there, she stood facing out over the ocean, her arms extended behind her, her hands holding the pier railing as she scanned the rolling waves.

"See him?" the mother cried, pointing at a spot in the dark sea.

"I see him." Amy leapt from the pier and plunged into the water.

Cold salt water hit Amy and enveloped her body. No matter how many times she jumped into the sea, the cold water was always a shock. She kicked to the surface of the rolling ocean and looked toward the pylons where the mother had pointed and where she had seen the boy. But she didn't see him now that the waves were at eye level and blocking her view.

It was so hard to see. The light from the lamp posts didn't reach far enough to help much. Was that pylon the one where he had been? Or had a wave swept him under the pier? In this dim light, it would be impossible to see much of anything under there. She hoped he was still by the pylon, because there was no time to waste. Swimming closer, she took a deep breath and dove down, reaching, blinding reaching...

Her fingers brushed something soft. She grasped it, only to realize it was a strand of seaweed. Her fear for the boy was rising. She continued to reach through the water. Where was he? If only it weren't so dark. He had been on the surface just seconds ago, so he couldn't have dropped very far. She was going to need to get some air soon. Her fingers brushed something soft again. Fabric? Yes! She grabbed hold and felt the connected weight of a small person. Her lungs beginning to burn, she secured him and kicked to the surface.

Breaking the surface of the water with the boy, she sucked in a much-needed breath of air. Cheering erupted on the pier, but she ignored it, worried about the limp body in her arms. Had the boy only now lost consciousness, or had it happened sooner? Had he suffered an injury from his entry into the water, had he been tossed against the pylon and hit his head, or had he simply tired from resisting the power of the waves? So many questions, and these dark, crashing waves by the pylons were no place to try to assess him, or if needed, to resuscitate him. She began swimming to shore as swiftly and carefully as she could.

Upon seeing Amy surface with the boy and start swimming to shore, Sarah sagged with relief. The frantic mother blinked away her tears and pressed her hands to her chest, a heartbreaking look of hope on her face. She and the crowd moved along the pier, following the progress of the swim to shore.

Eager to get down to the beach to help Amy if she could, Sarah bent to take off her sandals so she would be able to run faster. To the side near the railing, she noticed Amy's discarded sweater and belted slacks. Sandals in hand, she collected them along with Amy's dress socks and polished loafers.

A siren wailed in the distance—maybe the ambulance was coming. The sooner the better. Hugging the bundle of clothes and shoes to her chest, Sarah ran barefoot down the cold concrete and then descended the stairs to the beach.

On the beach, the only light was that cast from the lamp posts on the pier, which made it difficult to see very far into the distance. Leaving the bundle of clothes and shoes on the sand, Sarah ran closer to the water to try to see Amy. There she was—rapidly swimming through the waves with the boy in tow. Even in the dim light, Sarah could see the effort and determination on her face. Time was obviously of the essence—maybe the boy was hurt.

Could Amy use help getting him out of the water, or would she just want Sarah to stay out of the way? Sarah took a chance and waded into the surf toward them, the cold water swirling around her legs.

Amy reached shallower water and lifted the boy out of the surf. He looked limp, and Amy was carrying him in a way that looked as if she might be trying to minimize movement of his head and upper body. The muscles in her shoulders and arms stood out with the effort of maintaining the position.

"Do you want me to help you carry him?" Sarah shouted over the sound of the ocean.

Between panting breaths Amy spoke as she continued to hurry to shore. "I've got his torso. I don't know if he has a spinal injury from his fall. You can support his legs, but be careful to keep them aligned. Help me get him to the firmer sand just out of the water."

"Okay," Sarah said. Quickly grasping but carefully holding the boy's legs, she kept in step with Amy.

Was he going to need resuscitation? Amy could undoubtedly handle any CPR herself, but Sarah maintained a certification in basic life support as required for her job at South Coast Middle School. As they hurried up the shore, she spoke up, informing Amy of her training and her willingness to assist with CPR if needed.

"We'll have to modify for his possible injury, so I'll handle CPR, but it would be great if you could hold his head and neck stable on the sand because I won't be tilting his head back for the breathing—I'll only move his jaw."

"Okay," Sarah said. The sound of the sirens was closer, thank goodness.

They quickly lay the unmoving boy out on the sand and knelt beside him. Amy leaned down to do a quick assessment. "Not breathing," she announced. "No pulse," she announced. "Beginning CPR." She began compressions on his small chest while Sarah kept his head and neck stable.

The crowd had gathered again but was staying back. The mother was there, holding her toddler and looking on with wide, frightened eyes.

Having completed a round of compressions, Amy grasped the boy's jaw and lifted it forward without disturbing his neck, bent, gave him two rescue breaths, and immediately resumed compressions. Midway through the compressions, a wet, spasmy cough erupted from the boy.

"Help me turn him!" Amy said.

They rolled him to the side while keeping his head and torso aligned. The boy heaved up a large amount of water, coughing several times. He started crying.

Sarah had never been happier to hear a child crying. Now that the boy was awake and breathing on his own, maybe he would be okay. She looked to Amy. Amy met her gaze, relief apparent in her expression as well. In the periphery, the flashing lights of emergency vehicles appeared.

* * *

At the valet stand back at the restaurant, they waited in the now cool night air for the remaining valet on duty to bring Amy's SUV around. Amy wrapped her arms around Sarah to help keep her warm. The thin, shiny, plastic sheeting of the emergency blanket that the paramedics had given Sarah and which she wore like a shawl over her sleeveless dress made crinkling sounds as Amy held her. The bottom half of her dress was wet from the surf and looked to be clinging coldly to her legs. Amy felt her shiver. She wished the valet would hurry up. Sarah had had to sit in this uncomfortable ensemble while they had answered questions for the responding police officer's report and been checked by the paramedics.

Amy was cold, too, but at least she was wearing dry pants and a dry sweater. "Thanks again for bringing my clothes down from the pier," she said. "It would have been really unpleasant to wait for the valet in my bra and underwear. Not to mention that I would have had to give my report on the beach only half-dressed and wrapped in shiny sheeting."

"Of course," Sarah said. "Although, I imagine it was only slightly less unpleasant to give your report while wearing a cold, sodden bra and cold, wet underwear under those clothes."

Amy chuckled. "You might be right." She pressed a kiss to Sarah's hair.

The valet pulled up. Unwrapping her arms from Sarah, Amy hurried over to open the passenger door for her.

"Thanks." Sarah slid in, and Amy closed the door.

Amy met the valet, passed him his tip, and got in the driver's seat.

Sarah watched the valet depart. "The look the valet gave us was priceless," she said with a laugh.

"It was," Amy said, laughing, too. She reached for the temperature controls and turned up the heat. "I hope he won't mind if we stay parked here for a moment while we thaw." She held her hands in front of the vent for warmth.

Sarah did the same. "Oh, that feels good." She shrugged out of the emergency blanket.

Amy sighed. "Obviously, this wasn't quite the date that I had planned."

Sarah turned to her. "No. Don't you try to apologize," she said with quiet firmness. She took Amy's face between her hands and looked intently into her eyes. "What you did out there was incredible." She gave her a quick, fierce kiss. "I think you're amazing, and I couldn't have asked for a better date."

Amy lost herself in Sarah's eyes, moved by the depth of feeling that she saw there. "I'm so glad," she said softly, feeling her eyes mist now that the emotion and stress of the evening was hitting her. "Don't forget—you helped, too. We make a good team."

"You're being modest. I don't want to think about what might have happened to that boy if you hadn't been there."

Sarah pulled Amy closer for a hug, as close as the console between them would allow.

Amy hugged her back. She didn't want to think about what might have happened either. She was grateful the boy was all right or that he appeared to be so far. The paramedics hadn't identified any immediate problems other than mild hypothermia. They'd loaded him into the ambulance and taken him to the hospital, where a more detailed evaluation could be done. His mother had climbed into the back of the ambulance with her other child to ride with him.

Sarah straightened from the hug. "I guess I better let you start driving before the valet gets too anxious."

Amy released Sarah reluctantly. She put the vehicle in gear but kept her foot on the brake, hesitating. She didn't know if she should take Sarah home with her to her condo as planned or if Sarah would just like to be dropped off at her own home now. She turned toward her, the question on the tip of her tongue.

"I'm not tired—in case you were wondering, that is," Sarah said with a smile.

Amy grinned. "Good, I'm not tired, either." She put on her turn signal and headed for her condo.

Amy unlocked the condo, ushering Sarah in and flipping on the lights. After closing and locking the door, she turned around to find Sarah in the middle of a yawn. It immediately triggered the yawn that she herself had been suppressing. They stared at each other for a moment and then both burst into laughter.

"Maybe we're more tired than we thought," Sarah said.

"Maybe. Although I think I'm more hungry than tired. I could use a sandwich."

"Me too! Is that crazy? I didn't want to say anything because I was afraid you would think I was nuts after that three-course dinner we ate."

"No, don't worry about it." Amy squeezed Sarah's shoulder reassuringly. "It's from the cold and the stress. It burns a lot of calories."

"Okay, I feel a little less crazy then."

"Good." Amy smiled at her.

"But I don't think our outfits are suitable to wear at a second meal tonight, even if is here at the condo." Sarah looked down at herself, plucking at her damp dress, and then looked at Amy. She stepped closer to Amy and plucked at her sweater where moisture showed through from her wet bra. Some sand fell to the floor.

Amy chuckled. "Maybe not. What say we shower and then eat?"

"I thought you'd never ask."

They headed into the master bathroom. Sarah caught a glimpse of herself in the mirror. Her hair was wild and there were splotches of sand here and there. "Oh! It's even worse than I thought!"

Amy made a show of studying her. "No, I disagree. I think the bits of sand add a certain sparkle to your skin."

Sarah laughed and slapped playfully at her shoulder. More sand fell, and Amy laughed, too. "It's definitely time to get out of these clothes." She started undressing alongside her.

They shared the shower, mostly keeping their hands to themselves, both wanting to get warm and clean again and then get to the kitchen for a snack. First to exit from the shower, Amy toweled off and put on a robe. She hastened to the living room to turn on the fireplace to heat up while Sarah finished in the shower. The gas flames started with a reassuring *whoosh*. She stood in front of the screen, enjoying the gradually increasing heat that radiated from it.

Sandy lifted her head and regarded her sleepily from her blanket on the couch. She stretched, hopped down from the couch, wove around Amy's legs, and lay down in front of the fire. Amy petted her and then went into the kitchen to survey the refrigerator contents for sandwich fixings.

At the sound of Sarah's approach, she turned. "I have turkey lunch meat and cheese, or I have peanut butter and jelly."

"Turkey and cheese sounds good," Sarah said.

"I think I'll have that, too." She started pulling the food out of the refrigerator. "I can make our sandwiches. Why don't you go ahead and have a seat on the couch in front of the fire?"

"Okay," she said. "And I'd like my sandwich with a little mustard and mayonnaise, please."

"I can handle that. I'm going to have some orange juice, too. Would you like some?"

"Sure," she said over her shoulder. She took a seat on the couch and Amy heard her say "hi" to Sandy. Amy watched as Sandy got up from the floor and jumped onto her lap. Sarah started petting her, and Sandy started kneading her front paws into the fabric of Sarah's robe.

Amy smiled at the sight. It was so great to have Sarah here in her home. Sarah made her happy. When she thought of how she had avoided inviting her here earlier in their relationship, she wanted to kick herself. She finished making the sandwiches and carried them on plates into the living room. She set them on the coffee table and returned with the glasses of juice.

"Thanks. This looks good." Sarah moved Sandy off her lap and over to her blanket. Sandy settled there without a fuss. "You're such a good kitty, Sandy." Sarah reached over and petted her once more.

"Yes, she is—unless she has to take medicine. I'm sure glad that's over." Amy shook her head.

Sarah chuckled. She picked up her sandwich and began eating.

Amy ate too. The juice and sandwich tasted good. She settled back on the couch, plate in hand as she ate, taking occasional glances at Sarah. In the light of the fireplace, her skin had a lovely soft glow to it. But she was staring absently into the fire while she ate, and Amy wondered what she was thinking.

After a moment, Sarah turned to face her. "Were you scared out there?"

Amy finished the bite she was chewing. "Scared for myself, you mean?"

Sarah nodded.

"Sure. It would be hard not to be—there's risk with any rescue. But everything happens so quickly that there's not much time to think about it, and training just kicks in. Ultimately, I was more scared for the boy than for myself."

Sarah returned her gaze to the fire and spoke again. "It all happened so unbelievably quickly. One second he was on the railing, the next second he was gone—into that cold, dark water crashing around the pylons. And you went right after him. I was scared for both of you."

Amy scooted closer to her and wrapped her in a hug. Sarah held onto her and gave a small sniffle that tugged at her heart. Amy wanted to tell her it was okay, but she didn't want to offer platitudes since Sarah had seen what her job could be like. Instead, she said, "You were brave out there, and I felt lucky to have you with me." And it was true. Sarah was someone Amy would feel lucky to have by her side in any crisis. Amy eased back so that she could look into her eyes. "It feels nice that you worried about me," she said softly. "Just promise me that you won't worry too much. It's not every day that I have to do something like I did tonight."

Sarah sniffed again but nodded. "Okay. I'll try."

"Good, I don't want you to worry," she said, releasing her.

Sarah took a sip of orange juice and then went back to eating her sandwich. Amy did the same. Sarah seemed to have composed herself but stayed quiet while she ate, seeming lost in thought again. She finished her sandwich.

"If you're still thinking about everything that happened this evening, I'd be happy to talk more about all of it if that would make it easier," Amy said.

"No, that's okay. I wasn't still worrying. Not right now, anyway. I'm okay," Sarah gave a brief smile and touched Amy's hand as if to reassure her.

"Good, I'm glad." Amy finished the last bite of her sandwich. "Just let me know if you change your mind and want to talk more."

"Well…there was one thing I was still thinking about."

A playful quality in Sarah's tone made Amy look over at her. Maybe she really was feeling okay now. She had a teasing gleam in her pretty brown eyes and a corner of her mouth had quirked up. Amy liked that look; it usually led to good things.

Amy smiled and matched her playful tone to ask, "And what exactly is it that you're still thinking about?"

"I was wondering if that midnight blue bra and matching high-cut briefs you were wearing out there were specially chosen for our date tonight."

Amy grinned. Sarah was indeed feeling better. "I might have worn them with you in mind. But you never know." She shrugged. "After all, there's nothing like wearing lingerie to a rescue."

"You can say that again." Sarah fanned herself dramatically. "When you stripped down to those sexy panties and bra, there was a split second where I had completely inappropriate thoughts before I went back to worrying about you and worrying about the boy. You looked like a goddess standing out there on the edge of the pier. What's more, I had wanted you all through dinner."

Amy felt her face grow warm from her compliments. "I'm glad to know that I wasn't the only one having cravings for more than food during dinner."

Sarah smiled, moved closer, and Amy's pulse quickened. "You aren't wearing those panties and bra now, but that's okay because I still have a very good mental picture. Let me show you how well I remember." Sarah spread Amy's robe apart and planted a kiss along the top of one of her breasts and then gently pushed Amy back to lie on the couch, moving on top of her.

Disrupted by their movements, Sandy jumped down from the couch and left the room. Amy made a mental note to reward her with some of her favorite cat treats later.

"I think the cups curved something like this," Sarah said before she began kissing and licking her way across one of Amy's breasts, stopping between her breasts to plant another kiss and then making her way with her lips and tongue slowly across the other breast.

"Mmm, you have a good memory," Amy said. "Maybe you could show me again."

Sarah chuckled and then thumbed Amy's hard nipples, making her gasp in pleasure.

"Or you could keep doing that," Amy said with a smile. "But I want to feel all of you against me." She pushed at Sarah's robe and Sarah sat up to shrug out of it. Amy sat up also and slid her own robe the rest of the way off.

Sarah gazed at her and Amy felt her nipples tighten even more.

"I love your breasts," Sarah said, dipping her head to kiss one and pushing her to the couch again, seemingly intent on resuming where she had left off. Amy was only too happy to let her. Her nipples were achingly tight and begging for more of Sarah's touch. Sarah took one firm bud in her mouth and tongued it and then tongued it some more. Amy moaned. Sarah moved to the other and lavished it with the same attention. The intensity of the sensations was making Amy's center throb.

Amy pulled her up for a kiss. When Sarah's thigh pressed against her center, she moaned in pleasure. She held tighter and tilted her hips for more.

"Not just yet. I've only shown you my memory of you in that lovely bra, and I want to show you my memory of you in those high-cut briefs."

Amy loosened her hold, more than willing to cooperate.

Sarah gave her another kiss and made her way downward, trailing her kisses across her jaw to the sensitive area below her ear, lingering there before kissing, licking, and gently sucking her way down her neck and then down her torso, all of it making Amy's abdomen tighten with her gathering need.

"Now, the panties…it seems like they rested on your hip right about here…" Sarah placed her warm mouth on the front of Amy's hip, giving it a lick and a kiss. She softly dragged her warm tongue down the angle of her hip crease and then inward, just shy of her clit. She paused, hovering over her clit, her warm breath making it throb. She repeated her licks and kisses, this time from the other side, again pausing over her clit.

Amy felt so hard she could barely breathe. When Sarah lowered her mouth and enveloped her, she groaned from her depths and fought not to come right then. Sarah seemed to sense it and started softly. She lapped lightly against her, pausing and receding each time, like small waves at the shore. But the rhythmic motion was rapidly wearing away at her ability to hold on. When she changed to a swirling motion around her, like the flow of a surging tide, Amy clenched her hands on one of the robes beneath them. Sarah's tongue had her on the crest of a powerful wave. She cried out as her orgasm forcefully rolled through her.

Sarah waited a moment and then moved up and fitted herself next to her on the couch.

Amy tried to slow her breathing. "God, Sarah…" She looked over at her.

Sarah smiled at her.

After taking another moment to collect herself, she eased on top of Sarah. She wanted to make Sarah feel as good as she had made her feel and to show Sarah how much she was already coming to mean to her.

CHAPTER THIRTEEN

After spending Friday night and most of Saturday with Amy, it almost felt strange to Sarah to be in her own home this Sunday morning. She wandered into the kitchen to make herself breakfast. Her roommates had left on their commutes to their early shifts at the hospital a couple of hours ago, so she had the kitchen to herself.

As she set about the routine of making coffee, she found herself humming happily as she thought of Amy. She was falling for her, that was for sure. Did Amy feel the same about her? Sarah thought so. Amy's tender kisses and long, slow strokes in front of the fireplace a couple of nights ago had the feel of lovemaking—not just sex. There had been a new intimacy to lying in each other's arms afterward as well.

Saturday morning hadn't been quite as peaceful, though. The ringing of Amy's landline phone had woken them up at an early hour. Amy hadn't recognized the number on the caller ID display and so had let the call go to the answering machine. The call had been from a reporter who had left a message that he wanted to interview Amy about the pier rescue. That was only the first of the calls and messages; the phone had continued to ring with more unrecognized numbers and the answering machine had begun to fill up.

Amy hadn't been interested in any of the requests. When Sarah asked why, she said that she didn't like the idea of someone trying to single out one rescue as being worthier of a story than any other rescues that happened on a given day at the beach. She said the reporters would be able to get their quotes about the rescue from the department spokesperson. Then, she had taken Sarah out to breakfast so they could get away from the phone.

While the coffee brewed, Sarah took a couple of eggs and a leftover potato out of the refrigerator. She began grating the potato for hash browns. What if the phone started ringing here like it had at Amy's condo? Hopefully it wouldn't. The phone number was under Fiona's name, not Sarah's, so maybe the reporters wouldn't know to try calling here. They were resourceful, though, and worked fast. Amy had said her landline number was unlisted, but they had been able to call her the very morning after the rescue.

The phone rang, startling Sarah. The reporters were even more resourceful than she had imagined if they were already able to figure out she was at Fiona's number. She wasn't against granting them an interview about the rescue since she was proud of Amy and thought that she deserved the publicity, but she wasn't going to answer the calls if Amy didn't particularly want the attention.

She checked the phone's caller ID display in case it wasn't a reporter. *Oh—it was Justin.* Why was he calling so early and on the landline? Maybe he'd already tried her cell phone. Sarah set down the partially grated potato, wiped her hands, and picked up the phone. "Hello?"

"So," Justin answered, "I'm sitting here looking at my e-edition of the South Coast Beach Tribune, and who do I read about but you and your superhero girlfriend! All I've done so far on my summer vacation is watch movies, and here you are rescuing a little boy!"

"Oh, the rescue is in today's paper?" Sarah asked. She still needed to retrieve her copy of the paper from the driveway. If the story had made it into today's paper, hopefully she wouldn't need to worry about reporters calling.

"Yeah, the story is on the front page," he said. "The rescue sounds pretty amazing."

"It was," she said. "It was all Amy, but I did what I could to help." She told him some of the details.

"I'm not sure I would have been able to keep it together during all of that," he said.

"Yeah, it was hard to stay calm. The whole thing was really stressful, to say the least. Does the article say if the boy is all right? They carted him away in the ambulance for evaluation. Other than being cold and frightened, he seemed fine, but we didn't know if he suffered any lasting injuries from his fall."

"The article says he's fine. It says he was evaluated at SCB Hospital and then released."

"That's wonderful news," she said. They spoke a little longer. After ending the call, she put on a robe and went outside to get the paper.

She sat at the table to read the article. It was a little surreal to read about herself and Amy in an article like this, but it was a nice story and seemed to get the details of the rescue right. Especially nice were the quotes from Peter and other members of lifeguard management, all of whom had flattering things to say about Amy. Sarah got out her cell phone and texted Amy about the article.

Amy came in from reading the Sunday paper on her balcony to refill her coffee mug. Her phone chimed with a notification. It was a text from Sarah: *An article about my girlfriend is on the front page of today's paper!*

Amy grinned. She texted back: *What a coincidence—an article about my girlfriend is on the front page of today's paper, too!*

Her phone rang while she still held it in her hand and she looked at the display, thinking it must be Sarah deciding to call this time with her reply, but it was Aurora.

Aurora had likely seen the article, too. Their parents as well. What did they all think? She wasn't sure she wanted to find out. For all she knew, they would demand that she quit her lifeguard job now that they realized what it sometimes entailed. She debated whether to ignore the call but figured that Aurora would just call back later if she didn't pick up. "Hello?"

"Amy! The newspaper says you saved someone's life!"

"Well—"

"That's incredible! Why didn't you tell any of us?"

Amy didn't bother answering that. Surely, Aurora knew that everyone's lack of interest in her new job had dampened her enthusiasm for talking about her activities with them.

"Were you waiting until brunch to say something about it?" Aurora persisted.

Amy snorted. That was hardly the reason, and Aurora must know it. "I'm not coming to brunch."

"You already missed brunch last week. Are you still mad?"

Amy sighed. "Last week was Memorial Day weekend. I was working." Why couldn't any of her family remember that she now often worked weekends, not to mention holidays?

"You're not still mad, then?"

"Yes, I'm still mad! Why wouldn't I be? Dad and the rest of you think my job is to 'hang out' at the beach."

"That was just a misunderstanding."

"No, I understood very clearly."

"I think Dad was just upset. I think he feels a little rejected that you want to sell your dealership."

"Funny—rejected is how I've been feeling," Amy said. "And anyway, how rejected can he feel about it? It's not as though the dealerships were a family legacy we were expected to carry on. Neither you nor I have kids, after all. Someone else will eventually take over your dealership, too."

"Yeah, but the business is still his baby."

"Exactly. It's *his* baby. I have my own hopes and dreams."

Aurora was quiet for a moment. "Don't you miss your dealership at all?"

"No, I really don't. I love being a lifeguard. I should have done it sooner."

Aurora paused again. "Then I'll do what I can to help you find a buyer for your dealership if you still want to sell it."

She could hardly believe her ears. Maybe she had finally gotten through to a member of her family. "Yes—that would be great! I could use everyone's help to find a buyer. I put ads in the trade journals, but they won't be out until the next issues. I also listed the dealership on a couple of websites."

"I'll see what I can do," Aurora said. "Speaking of which, why weren't you quoted in that article in the paper today?"

"What?" Amy asked.

"Didn't the reporter try to contact you?"

"Yes, but I thought I would just let the department handle it."

"Well, you should reconsider. Give the reporter a call, and let him do a story on you. Tell him about owning a car dealership that you're trying to sell, so you can keep being a lifeguard."

"Oh," Amy said. "That's a good idea. I guess I should do that. Thanks, Aurora."

"And get the rest of us Bergens who are trying to sell cars some publicity, too."

Amy snorted again. "Now that's the Aurora I know," she teased—though she wasn't entirely joking. She should have known that part of Aurora's motivation for calling was to find a way to horn in on Amy's publicity, but she'd let it slide since her sister appeared to be coming around to her side.

"Ha, ha," Aurora teased her back. "So who's this girlfriend the article mentioned? Are you going to bring her to brunch? You are coming to brunch now, right?"

"I'll think about coming to brunch. But as for Sarah, I really like her and I'm not sure I want to subject her to brunch while selling my dealership is still a source of discord at the table. The last thing I need is for the Bergen family brunches to scare her off."

Not long after Amy finished the phone call with Aurora, her mother and father called. She had similar conversations with them. It was a start. She got dressed and drove over for brunch.

CHAPTER FOURTEEN

Sarah closed her laptop with a frustrated snap and sagged in her chair at her kitchen table. It had been a month and a half since the rescue and people were still posting and commenting all over social media on pictures of Amy in her bra and underwear. Bystanders with cameras and cell phones had captured her in photos and video that night, and some of the posts had gone viral. Although many of the photos and videos were not very clear because of the dim light at the time, Amy's fit, lingerie-clad body could still be seen as the object of beauty that it was, especially as she stood preparing to jump into the water.

Sarah wanted to think that people were posting and viewing the videos on the websites only to see a difficult and daring rescue performed, but the comments on the websites told her that the majority of viewers were interested in Amy herself and not in a platonic way. According to the counts on the various sites, the videos had been viewed thousands of times, which meant thousands of pairs of hungry eyes had feasted on the images of her girlfriend in her lingerie.

Amy's recent interview on a popular daytime television talk show that taped in Hollywood would probably prolong the circulation of the photos and videos even more. The interviews she had given earlier in local and regional newspapers and on the local evening news had certainly had that effect.

Sarah kept reminding herself that the media attention was actually a good thing because Amy was using it to create more awareness that her dealership was for sale. But what the media attention was also doing was attracting groupies to Amy. Sarah had heard some of the X-rated messages they left on Amy's answering machine. She wished she could unhear them. Determined groupies were competition no one in a relationship needed and Sarah was doing her best not to worry that Amy would be tempted by any of it.

Amy professed to be averse to lifeguard groupies or uniform chasers, but ever since she had decided to cooperate with reporters and other members of the media after the rescue, she had been rather busy on her days off and even during some of her evenings. On the Sundays she wasn't scheduled to work, she was busy with those family brunches that Sarah wondered if she would be inviting her to anytime soon.

Sarah trusted her, but with their recent lack of time together it was hard not to let her imagination run away with thoughts of her and other women. The fact that her own schedule was completely open, now that school was out for the summer, made Amy's lack of availability even more noticeable.

Abruptly, Sarah stood up from the kitchen table. She was going to take matters into her own hands and visit Amy at work today with a picnic lunch. Amy had to have time for lunch.

Sarah pedaled her bicycle in the direction of SCB Lifeguard Headquarters, first stopping at the Vietnamese food truck to collect an assortment of food which she loaded into her backpack to take for the meal with Amy. Much of the junior lifeguard program took place on the section of beach in front of headquarters, so Sarah hoped she would find Amy there. Pulling up in front of the beige stucco and stone building, she hopped off her bike and locked it to the building's crowded rack. The building was two stories tall and looked something like a larger version of the lifeguard towers on the beach, with its angled walls, prominent eaves, and large windows.

Sarah surveyed the section of beach in front of the building, looking for Amy. The beach was full of kids wearing red swim trunks or red swimsuits in the bright sunshine and there were a handful of adults among them wearing red and white colored lifeguard clothing. The kids' attention was on a small stage set up on the sand where some instruction appeared to be taking place. She didn't want to disrupt anything, but she needed to get a little closer if she was going to be able to spot Amy amidst the crowd of similarly dressed people. She started down to the beach with her backpack of food.

"Excuse me, ma'am," a male voice called out. "The public isn't allowed in this area right now."

Sarah stopped, preparing to explain herself to the man she assumed was a lifeguard since he was wearing red shorts and a white polo shirt with the SCB lifeguard emblem.

"It's okay, John," another male voice called out. "She's with me."

Sarah turned to see Peter approaching and smiled. "Hi, Peter."

"Hi. Here to see Amy?"

Before she could reply, the man named John snorted. "Isn't everyone?" he muttered and walked away.

She frowned. What was his problem? She looked at Peter, who was also frowning as he watched John's retreating form.

"Would you wait just a moment?" Peter touched Sarah's shoulder before walking swiftly after John. He caught up to him and began speaking in low tones. John looked chastened. Peter ended the conversation and walked back to Sarah. "I'm sorry about that. His comment was uncalled for. I didn't want to let it slide."

"What did he mean, anyway?"

Peter looked a little uncomfortable and didn't immediately answer.

"Oh—did he think I was with the media?"

"No..."

"What did he mean that everyone is here to see Amy, then?"

Peter sighed. "Well, there have been a certain number of... fans coming by."

"Groupies, you mean."

"Yes. John thought you were one of them."

Sarah hadn't realized people were coming to Amy's workplace. Why hadn't Amy mentioned this was happening? Justin's warnings about secrets suddenly surfaced in her mind, filling her with worry. "John seemed kind of resentful. Is it because the groupies are causing trouble, or is it because other lifeguards are feeling jealous of Amy?"

"No, I don't think any of them are jealous, not for the most part. Some who don't know her might be, but I think most understand that she's only courting the media attention to try to sell her dealership."

"I'm sure it's easy for her coworkers to get the wrong idea," Sarah said, "but she's given a lot of credit to the entire lifeguard team in the interviews and I know she would hate for anyone to be jealous."

"Yes, the publicity has been great for the department. Everyone here knows that, but there are always a few who will be envious."

"She's lucky to have a good friend like you in the department. I know you're part of the reason she got back into lifeguarding, so you must be very proud of her."

"I am," he said. "I'm very glad she's here. Did you know that the little boy she rescued told me he wants to be a lifeguard when he grows up?"

"Wow, that's great. Maybe when he's old enough, he can do the junior lifeguard program."

Peter smiled. "That's what I told him."

"So...I notice you didn't answer the part about whether the groupies have been causing trouble," she said gently. "Does that mean they have been?"

"They've eased up for the most part, but for a while there, they were bothersome. Only a few leave lingerie and notes anymore."

"What! They leave lingerie and notes?" Sarah felt sick. Why hadn't Amy told her any of this?

"Yeah, midnight blue lingerie like in the rescue photos."

Sarah's worries must have shown on her face, because Peter added, "But don't worry about it. Everything is beginning to quiet down, just like we thought it would."

Sarah took a breath. Maybe that's why Amy hadn't told her—because she thought the lingerie-leaving groupies were just a temporary situation. Or at least Sarah hoped that was why she hadn't said anything about it. Amy wouldn't cheat on her… would she?

Peter gave her shoulder a comforting squeeze. "Hey, it's okay. I didn't mean to stress you out."

"No, no, it's fine. You're right—things can only start to quiet down after being so hectic. That's why I came by today. I thought it would be good to join her for lunch."

He nodded. "Sure, the lunch break is coming up soon. But before that, you might like to see Amy teach the kids the stingray shuffle."

"The what?" Sarah asked. She was still worrying about the lingerie and the notes.

"Just watch," he said with a smile. He gestured to the small stage as Amy jogged up the few steps from the side of the platform and then strode to the middle to stand before the audience of kids. The kids quieted. They obviously knew and respected Amy. Sarah drank in Amy's fit, toned body as she held stage.

Amy picked up the microphone. "One of the things we want to teach you today is a dance," she said with a smile. "It's a nice little dance and very simple. I think you'll like it."

The kids in the audience murmured curiously, and her smile broadened.

"I bet you didn't think you would be learning to dance in the junior lifeguard program, did you?"

Kids laughed and gave answers of "Uh-uh."

"Well, this is not just any dance. It's a special dance." She paused, and the crowd leaned forward in anticipation. "We call this dance the stingray shuffle."

The kids repeated the phrase "stingray shuffle" in a curious murmur.

"Who remembers what a stingray is from our trip to the aquarium the other day?"

Kids called out answers. "That's right," Amy said, repeating and summarizing their answers. "And what do you think might happen if someone wading into the ocean stepped on a stingray that happened to be resting there in the shallow water?"

"They might get hurt from a sting!" the kids called.

"Yes. Getting stung really hurts and can be serious depending on how severe the reaction is or the health of the person who gets stung." Amy described some possible problems and complications. "That's why it's important that everyone learn the stingray shuffle. Doing the stingray shuffle will usually make the stingrays swim away. It's especially important to do on hot days like today when the ocean is warmer, because that's when the stingrays can be most plentiful near the shore." Amy put her hands on her hips and surveyed the crowd. "Are you ready to do the stingray shuffle?"

"Yeah!"

"Then let's shuffle! Everybody stand up!"

The kids stood up.

"The stingray shuffle goes like this," Amy said. She made a show of doing a silly shuffling movement, not fully lifting her feet, but rather scraping them around, as she moved on the stage. "That's all there is too it. Now you try."

The kids shuffled, laughing.

"That's great! Easy, right?" Amy shuffled some more, still holding stage.

After the kids seemed to have gotten their fill of shuffling, Amy spoke into the microphone again. "Now, the stingray shuffle only works if all the people on the beach remember to do it, so let's talk about first aid in case someone does get stung.

Lifeguards have a first aid bag for stingray stings." Amy held a bag up for the kids to see and then described soaking the sting in very warm water and other first aid measures to take. Wrapping up the session, she exited the stage.

Sarah turned to Peter. "You're right, I did like seeing that. Amy was great and she's a natural at teaching the kids."

"Yeah," he said, nodding and smiling. "Let me take you over to her now."

"Okay, because I had better have an escort so no one besides John thinks I'm a crazed groupie who might try to rush the stage," Sarah joked. She wasn't going to let the discovery about groupies flocking here ruin the lunch she had planned with Amy, but she didn't know how long she could wait to ask her about why she had been keeping it all a secret.

Amy turned at the sound of Peter's voice calling her name. He was walking toward her and Sarah was with him. Sarah's blond hair was glossy in the sunshine and windblown, as though she might have ridden her bike here. A backpack was slung over one shoulder. "Hi, Sarah!" she called with a smile and a wave and began walking toward them.

"Hi!" Sarah said, stopping before her with Peter.

"Is everything okay?" Amy asked. She glanced at Peter and back to Sarah. Everything seemed fine, but Sarah had never come here before.

"Yes, I just wanted to see you," Sarah said. "And I brought lunch." She patted the backpack slung over her shoulder.

Amy grinned. "It sounds like today is my lucky day, then—I wanted to see you too…and I'm hungry for lunch."

Peter chuckled. "It looks like my work here is done—I'll leave you two to your lunch."

"Thanks, Peter," Amy said. "I'll see you in a little while."

"Yes, thanks again, Peter," Sarah said.

"Sure thing." He smiled, gave a nod, and walked away.

"So, you brought lunch?" Amy asked.

"Yes, I brought some of our favorites from the food truck."

"Yum!" Amy said with a smile. "Why don't we walk down the block to where there are a couple of benches with a nice view? With any luck, one will be available and we can eat there."

"Sounds great—lead the way."

"Here, give me your backpack, and I'll carry it." Amy slipped the backpack off Sarah's shoulder and slung it over her own. She reached for her hand, clasping it, and they strolled the distance to the benches. Both benches were available. They chose one, and Amy handed the backpack to Sarah, who unzipped it and began extracting packages and containers.

"Here, these are chicken bánh mì," Sarah said, handing two paper-wrapped and taped bundles to Amy. "Why don't you unwrap them while I put together our salad?" She set out a container of green papaya salad and its accompanying container of vinaigrette and little packages of toppings of chopped peanuts and Vietnamese cilantro.

"Okay." Amy undid the tape and laid out the sandwiches on top of the wrappers. "Anything for dessert?" she asked hopefully.

"Of course," Sarah said. "I got us coconut custard." She added that to the assortment of food on the bench.

"You're awesome," Amy said, leaning over to give Sarah a kiss.

Sarah smiled. "And here are some ice teas," she said, reaching into her backpack once more and setting out two bottles.

Amy opened them both and handed one to her. She raised her bottle and tapped it to Sarah's. "Thanks for going to the trouble to do this. It's a treat to see you during my lunch break."

Amy hadn't seen nearly as much of Sarah as she would have liked lately, because talking with the media about the pier rescue and about her goal of selling her dealership had been keeping her busy. While the publicity was free, apart from the cost of her time, Amy was finding that the old saying "you get what you pay for" was unfortunately ringing true, because only a couple of people who had contacted her as a result of the publicity seemed legitimately interested in the dealership. But she had just done a TV talk show, so that should attract more interest. And there were still the ads she had placed in the trade journals, which should also attract interest.

"You're welcome." Sarah smiled. "It's a treat for me, too, and it was fun to watch you teach. I didn't know I was going to get to see you do that. I have to admit, it was a little bit of a turn-on for me."

"Oh? I didn't know you liked the stingray shuffle, or I would have demonstrated it sooner," Amy teased.

Sarah swatted at her. "You know what I mean. You, striding around on stage, taking charge, teaching the kids. I liked watching you."

"I'm glad," she said. She gazed at Sarah. She had known what Sarah meant. She thought Sarah looked sexy doing most anything. She reached out to caress her cheek.

Sarah blushed sweetly. "We should eat before you have to get back." She handed Amy a fork and offered her the freshly tossed green papaya salad.

She took a forkful and chewed. "Mmm." The crunchy, tangy salad was always tasty.

Sarah began to eat, too, taking bites of her sandwich and sharing the salad with her.

Amy relaxed in the warm sun as they ate. It had been a while since she had felt this free of tension. All of the time spent with the media in the last month and a half had been draining. Too much time spent schmoozing and interacting with demanding strangers always took a toll on her. It was probably one of the reasons that running an auto dealership had never been a good fit for her. She couldn't imagine going back to that and hoped her recent efforts with the media would result in some more sales leads.

Sarah looked out at the ocean as she ate and sipped from her bottle of tea, seemingly lost in her own thoughts as well, her long hair gently ruffling in the light sea breeze. Just when Amy was about to ask what she was thinking, Sarah turned to her and spoke. "How come you didn't tell me you have groupies coming to see you at work?"

Amy sat up. "Peter told you about that, huh?" Not that it was a secret, but she wished he hadn't said anything.

Sarah nodded. "But only because one of the other lifeguards thought I was one of your new fans. Why didn't you mention what was happening?"

Amy shrugged. "I didn't want to bother you with it. I know the social media stuff has been stressing you out and I didn't want to make it worse."

"Peter said people have been leaving lingerie and notes for you."

Amy shrugged again. "I've been trying to ignore all of it and hope that it goes away."

Sarah looked down.

"Hey," Amy said softly. She gently drew Sarah's face up with her hand until she was looking at her again. "I'm sorry I kept it from you. You don't have anything to worry about. You know that, right?"

"You're not tempted by all of it?"

"Tempted by some stranger's lingerie?" Amy shook her head. "No. You, however, tempt me a great deal."

Sarah gave her a small smile.

Amy leaned closer and kissed her. "If I didn't have to get back to work soon, I would take you home with me and show you just how much you tempt me."

"Really?"

"Really." Amy kissed her again. Those vapid and attention-seeking groupies had nothing on her smart, pretty, and kind-hearted girlfriend. If anything, Amy was worried that the groupies would scare Sarah away from her.

"Let's have dessert," Amy suggested. She handed her a spoon and kept the other for herself. She offered the container of coconut custard to Sarah, who took a spoonful, and then she took a spoonful too. The creamy custard was yummy, just like the rest of the lunch had been. After they finished, they gathered up the empty wrappers and packages from their lunch and put them in the nearby trash can. They started the walk back to headquarters.

Amy spoke. "I've been meaning to ask you—would you come to the Lifeguard Luau with me? It's in a couple weeks, on the last Saturday of the month."

"Sure, I'd love to…but maybe you could tell me what it is?" Sarah gave her a playful smile.

"Oh, right." Amy chuckled. It was easy to overlook the details when blissed out from a wonderful lunch and walk along the beautiful oceanfront with Sarah. "The Lifeguard Luau is another of our annual fundraisers. It's for the junior lifeguard program and our other community recreational activities and outreach programs."

"Great, I'd definitely love to go."

"Good, it will be fun."

Sarah stopped in front of the bike rack at headquarters. "This is me," she said, gesturing to her bike.

Amy nodded. She didn't want her to leave, but the lunch break was almost over. "What about tonight? Are you free tonight?" she asked.

"Why, what's tonight? Is there another media thing?"

"No, tonight is unfortunately how long I have to wait to thank you properly for this surprise visit today," she said with a salacious grin. "If you'll let me, that is."

Sarah grinned back. "It's a date."

CHAPTER FIFTEEN

From the passenger seat of Amy's SUV, Sarah watched the multimillion-dollar homes go by on the winding incline to the estate where the Lifeguard Luau was being held. Given the informal title of the event, Sarah had been surprised to learn that it was being held in this opulent area of the city, but apparently a wealthy retired actor who had made his money in beach films allowed his estate to be used each year as the location for this lifeguard department fundraiser.

Sarah hadn't been in this area of South Coast Beach since her time with Robin. It felt strange to be driving along these roads on a date with Amy. At least Amy took the curves at a more sensible speed that Robin ever had. Nevertheless, Sarah was clenching her hands to her thighs out of habit. She made herself relax, straightening her fingers and smoothing her dress.

"Am I driving too fast?" Amy asked. "I'll slow down."

"No, no, I'm fine. Just a little nervous, I guess," Sarah said, not wanting to mention Robin if she could avoid it.

"Oh, don't be. The Luau isn't anything formal, despite the neighborhood."

That might be true, but Sarah was glad she had worn a new dress for the occasion. She had gone shopping, sifting through various sale racks, and had the good fortune to happen upon a side-tie dress in a floral pattern that seemed perfect for tonight.

Amy, as usual, looked delectable. She wore a pale khaki, tailored linen suit that complemented her fit physique. Under the suit jacket, she wore a white cable knit sweater of a clingy thinness that curved over her breasts and snugged in at her trim abdomen. Sarah was already looking forward to time with her after the event.

After Amy parked, they walked some distance to arrive at the sprawling estate and followed signs and other attendees to a side gate leading to the back lawn where attendants stood collecting tickets. Polynesian music was playing, live from the sound of it. Amy reached inside her suit jacket and presented two tickets to the attendants, who smiled and welcomed them inside.

On a large patio overlooking the lawn, a band was set up, with the band members wearing Hawaiian shirts and leis. The lawn was dotted with brightly lit tiki torches and arrayed with tables and chairs. Light green tablecloths covered the tables and each table held a centerpiece of a hollowed-out pineapple base filled with flowers. The whole area was heady with the scent of flowers, and it wasn't just from the centerpieces. The arbor she and Amy walked under was covered in a fragrant and beautiful flowering vine, and many other flowers bloomed in the lush and verdant yard. "What an amazing yard," Sarah said.

"It is, isn't it?" Amy was admiring a grouping of bird of paradise plants with multiple exotic orange and violet flowers in bloom.

There were white tents on both sides of the yard. The caterers' tents were set up on one side. Sarah wondered what was being served in addition to something that likely involved the pineapple from the centerpieces. Next to the catering area, it looked like drinks were being served.

Amy followed her gaze. "Maybe we should head over and get something to drink. It's getting crowded."

"Okay. What's going on in those other tents?" She gestured to the opposite side of the yard.

"That's the silent auction. Some local businesses and a couple of athletes from the area have donated items and services to be auctioned as part of our fundraiser."

"That's nice of them. Can we check it out later?" There were a lot of people milling around in the tents. There must be some good things on offer.

"Definitely. There's always great stuff to bid on. And I'm curious to see how much the new set of performance tires I donated is going to bring in."

They got in line for the no-host bar which looked to be offering beer and wine.

"Sarah! Amy! Hi!"

They turned around to be pulled into a hug from Justin. "Fancy meeting you here!" He smiled at them. "And you know Ron," he said, indicating his boyfriend, who smiled and greeted them also.

"I didn't know we'd see you here," Sarah exclaimed happily.

"I go to the Luau every year," Ron said, "but this year I get to bring Justin." He gave him an affectionate smile.

Sarah smiled at him. Ron was a lot sweeter than the prima donnas Justin usually went out with. She was happy for Justin and hoped his relationship with Ron continued to go well. "We should sit together later," she said to them.

"Yes, let's," Justin said. "First, Ron and I are going to do a little dancing. I wonder if I can get the band to play some Don Ho. I like 'Tiny Bubbles.'" He and Ron headed off to the dance area in front of the patio.

Their confidence at venturing out among what currently seemed to be all heterosexual couples at the dance area impressed Sarah. She watched Justin and Ron for a while as she and Amy continued to wait in line. No one seemed to be giving them more than a glance. Maybe she and Amy would be able to dance, too. "It's a pretty nice crowd here," she commented.

"Yeah, it's always more pleasant when that's the case, isn't it?" Amy said, easily following her train of thought. She put her arm around Sarah and Sarah leaned into her while they continued to wait in line. At the bar, they got glasses of merlot and headed toward the silent auction area.

On the way over, they ran into some of Amy's fellow lifeguards and their dates. Amy introduced her and she and Amy joined in the conversation with everyone. With everyone chatting happily, Sarah was glad to see that the sour grapes lifeguard at Lifeguard Headquarters the other week seemed to be the exception as far as jealousy for Amy's success was concerned.

As the other lifeguards began talking more about work, some of their dates broke off together and headed toward the silent auction tents, gathering Sarah up with them on the way. Sarah looked back over her shoulder at Amy, who flashed her a smile while she stayed to finish chatting with her coworkers.

In the tent, Sarah and the other girlfriends began to check out the items up for bid. The first silent auction table seemed to have a sports theme. There was a can of tennis balls autographed by a famous tennis player. One of the women let out an excited cry and wrote down a bid. There was a golf club—a driver—donated by South Coast Beach Country Club, which Robin's best friend Samantha owned. Out of curiosity, Sarah looked at the value listed on the bid sheet. She sucked in a breath. Who knew a golf club cost that much? It must be something really high-tech. Samantha wasn't the generous type, so it was unlikely the donation had been made from the goodness of her heart; it was probably an attempt to lure some of the attendees into joining her country club. The next sheet listed a kayaking lesson. That could be fun.

The women moved onto the next table, and Sarah walked with them. Hmm, a whale-watching excursion. Sarah had seen advertisements for whale-watching tours when she had done some sightseeing along the wharf in another coastal city. She had been interested in going, but the tours were large group tours that involved someone speaking on a microphone to the crowd on the boat. It didn't seem like quite the experience she wanted, even though she would love to see a whale up close. This excursion, however, was by private charter boat and that interested her more. As to her budget, the minimum bid was steep, but it would be a lot of fun to go on a boat ride with Amy and have the chance to see a whale. Plus, it was for a good cause. She wrote her name down with the minimum bid on the bidding sheet.

"Oh, I don't think that bid is going to last long," a woman's voice said.

Sarah straightened from her writing and found herself face-to-face with Robin.

Robin smiled unpleasantly at her. "In fact, I know it's not going to last. Angelique likes whales, too, don't you, babe?" Robin glanced at the woman standing next to her but didn't wait for an answer before bending to write in a new bid that was several times the number listed as the minimum raise.

Sarah felt an all-too familiar tension creep into her body at Robin's comments. She wanted to walk away and ignore her, but the woman Robin had called Angelique was smiling expectantly at Sarah, so Sarah stayed and introduced herself.

Angelique shook her hand politely. She looked to be in her early twenties. She had long, wavy blond hair and a nicely made-up face and was wearing a snug and low-cut red tube dress. Even if Angelique was going to be the one who got to go on the whale-watching private charter, Sarah felt a little sorry for her that she would be going with Robin.

Robin looked Sarah up and down, no doubt judging her new dress. It was a look Sarah remembered well from her time with her and her friends, who all had the habit of assessing the worth of each other's attire and trying to one-up each other with the newest trends.

"Doing okay over here?" Amy asked as she walked over and slipped her arm around Sarah. She eyed Robin, clearly remembering her from the day at the coffeehouse.

"Fine," Sarah answered calmly. She didn't want to give Robin the satisfaction of letting her know that her little snipes were already making her tense. "I was just talking to my ex,

Robin, and her girlfriend Angelique. Robin, Angelique, this is my girlfriend, Amy."

"Pleased to meet you, Angelique," Amy shook her hand and gave her a smile. She glanced unsmiling at Robin. "I believe we've already met at a coffeehouse."

Robin grunted and looked away.

Angelique glanced between the two.

"What are you doing here, Robin?" Sarah asked.

Robin glanced over at Amy, looking her up and down with a sneer. "Supporting the city lifeguards, what else?"

Sarah rolled her eyes and waited, knowing that something selfless like that wouldn't be Robin's real reason.

Robin shrugged. "A lot of important people are here tonight—people who might need my talents as a realtor."

Sarah nodded. "I should have known that you came to network." And she knew that by "important," Robin meant people with money.

Robin shrugged again. "What can I say? I got a very nice commission out of that one," she said, gesturing at the sprawling mansion. "Who knows what opportunities might come my way tonight?"

Angelique, who had started to fidget in an excited manner during the conversation and who had fixed her gaze on Amy, spoke. "OMG! You're that lifeguard! I saw you on that talk show! You're the one who rescued that little boy!" Angelique was now hopping up and down—to the extent that her high heels allowed—and flapping her hands excitedly. Her squeals drew the attention of guests nearby. She pressed closer to Amy, as did other people, and Sarah was squeezed aside as they congratulated Amy and clamored for a firsthand recounting of the rescue.

"Looks like your girlfriend is the flavor of the month," Robin said, coming to stand by Sarah.

"Last month, too," Sarah said with a frustrated sigh before she could stop herself from responding to Robin's dig. Amy's popularity would be more tolerable if people had better boundaries.

Angelique edged even closer to Amy. One of her breasts appeared to be grazing Amy and she rested her hand on Amy's arm as she listened to her speak. Sarah was quickly realizing that Angelique wasn't the innocent lamb she appeared to be.

A muscle pulsed in Robin's jaw as she watched Angelique and Amy, but her eyes were mostly on Amy, giving Sarah the impression that Robin wasn't so much concerned with Angelique's blatant flirting but rather with Amy's ability to draw so much attention. As Amy collected what looked like a business card or two from the crowd and slipped them into her pocket, Sarah could see Robin practically turn green with envy.

"Ladies and gentlemen…" A voice came over the sound system and made an announcement that the caterers were ready to start serving dinner. People began making their way over to the catering tents to line up at the serving area, and the crowd around Amy dispersed. Angelique had little choice but to relinquish her space next to her and return to Robin. Robin and Angelique headed for the catering area.

Amy came to stand by Sarah. "Sorry about all of that," she said, looking embarrassed.

"It's okay," Sarah said. "You might as well network while the opportunity presents itself."

"Thanks," Amy said. She squeezed Sarah's hand. "I did make a couple of contacts."

"That's good."

Amy nodded. "Are you ready to go see what they're serving for dinner?"

"Yes, and let's sit far away from Robin and Angelique."

Amy laughed. "No problem."

The line for dinner moved quickly. Amy and Sarah gathered their food and drink and then scanned the area for Justin and Ron.

"There they are," Sarah said. She gestured with a little tilt of her chin, as her hands were full with her plate and her drink. "Oh, and that's Peter with them. It'll be fun to sit with everyone."

"Yes, I see them. And that's Peter's wife, Tammy. I'll introduce you."

Tammy was nice, like Peter, and Sarah enjoyed getting to chat with everyone during dinner. Conversation flowed easily among the group and the food was good. Dinner was roast pork, rice pilaf, tropical coleslaw, and a dinner roll. It was a simple meal but well-prepared and satisfying. The dessert course, on the same plate, consisted of a cute miniature lava cake.

The tropical coleslaw, in particular, was tasty. Amy seemed to be enjoying it, too. Sarah wondered if she could replicate the dish at home the next time she had Amy over. It appeared to be regular coleslaw with the addition of diced pineapple, diced mango, and chopped green onions. It had a little zip to it, too, so maybe there was a bit of cayenne in the dressing. Maybe they could make it together like they did salsa, adjusting the ingredients and seasonings until it came out just right.

"Ladies and gentlemen..." The announcer's voice came over the sound system again at a break in the band sets. He announced that the silent auction would remain open for the next two hours and encouraged everyone to place their bids and to take advantage of the live music for dancing until the winners would be announced. He also announced that coffee was now available in the catering area.

Sarah offered to get coffee for the group and roped Justin into helping her so she could talk to him privately. "I didn't want to bring it up in front of the others and ruin the dinner conversation, but Robin's here."

"No—tell me she isn't," Justin said.

"Yes, I'm afraid it's true. I ran into her at the silent auction, where she promptly outbid me on something."

"What a bitch." He shook his head.

"Yeah, and she's with a gem of a girlfriend. Angelique is her name."

"Angelique, huh?"

Sarah nodded. "She was so star-struck when she figured out who Amy was that I thought she was going to ask Amy to autograph her boobs."

Justin snorted, but Sarah had only been partly joking.

"Anyway, be on the lookout for a blonde in a red tube dress and steer clear. I know I'm going to."

"You and me both," he said.

She and Justin gathered cups of coffee at the catering tent and returned to the table. A round of "thanks" was murmured as everyone accepted the coffee. Sarah sat back down next to Amy and they sipped theirs. People from some of the nearby tables had begun making their way to the dance area.

A woman's manicured finger slithered across Amy's shoulder. "Can I have this dance, stud?"

Sarah looked up at the woman whose hand was on her girlfriend. Samantha! God, was she here, too?

Samantha winked at her. Sarah took a deep breath.

Amy craned her head around to see whose hand was on her.

"I almost didn't recognize you with your clothes on," Samantha said as she looked down at Amy, her hand still on her shoulder.

"Excuse me?" Amy asked.

"Oh, that came out wrong," Samantha said with another wink at Sarah before turning back to Amy. "I was referring to those videos of the rescue."

Samantha's attempt to sound apologetic wasn't fooling Sarah. This was one of her cleverly planned incursions—Sarah remembered them all too well. She sensed Justin, Ron, Peter, and Tammy looking at them. She wanted to head Samantha off before she became any more provocative or embarrassing. "Everyone, this is Samantha, a friend of my ex's. She owns the South Coast Beach Country Club."

Samantha spared the group a glance and greeting.

"Oh, you donated that beautiful new driver for the silent auction," Peter said.

"Why, yes, I did donate that. It is a beautiful club, isn't it?"

Peter nodded. "Very generous of you. Our department appreciates it."

Samantha smiled and turned her attention back to Amy. "So how about that dance?" She slithered her finger along Amy's shoulder again.

Amy took a breath. She cast a baleful look at Peter and then turned to Sarah. "Do you mind? I won't be long."

"Oh, I don't know about that," Samantha said in sultry tones before Sarah could answer. "I think we'll have lots to talk about, maybe even about that dealership of yours." She took Amy's arm and led her away.

"Well," Justin said.

"Yeah," Sarah said. She got up, not wanting to discuss Samantha with anyone. "I think I'm going to get another coffee. The rest of you should go ahead and dance, too."

"Are you sure?" Justin asked.

"Yes. I'm sure Amy will be back for me soon." Sarah headed for the catering tent.

After clearing her head with the walk for another coffee, she headed back to the now empty table. She sat down alone and watched the dancing.

She easily spotted Samantha, who was wearing a white dress that stood out against the other, more colorful dresses on the other women. It was a one-shoulder dress with a slit up one leg that showed off her country club tan in the light from the tiki torches. Like Robin, she was older, but Samantha was fitter and trimmer from her constant golfing and easily pulled off wearing a dress in that revealing style.

Sarah didn't like what she was seeing on the dance floor. It didn't look like any kind of business discussion was taking place between Samantha and Amy out there. What was happening was that Samantha was feeling Amy up. Her hands were everywhere, squeezing a bicep here, caressing a shoulder there, and getting dangerously close to her breasts.

Sarah wanted to step in. But on the off chance that Samantha really was interested in Amy's dealership, she wasn't going to break up the dance. That, and Samantha was a donor at this event, which Peter clearly appreciated. Sarah sighed.

Robin approached the table. "Looks like your girlfriend is busy again. How about a dance?"

Sarah had no interest in dancing with Robin. "Why don't you dance with Angelique?"

"She seems to have wandered off while I was busy taking a call."

"You and your cell phone," Sarah said.

"Business is business. You had more patience than she does."

"I shouldn't have been as patient as I was. You weren't very nice a lot of the time." She wished Robin would go away.

"I was nice. I bought you things. For most women, that's enough."

Sarah shook her head. They'd been through this before. "Maybe Angelique wouldn't wander off if you did more than just buy her things."

Robin shrugged. "Maybe, maybe not. Angelique is easily drawn to novel things," she said with a casual look at the dance area.

Something in her tone made Sarah look as well. She barely held back a gasp. Angelique was there with Amy, dancing with her and twining her arms around her like an invasive, creeping vine. When had she gotten out there, and where had Samantha gone off to? Samantha was bad enough, but Angelique was worse and even more dangerous than Sarah thought if she had managed to cut in on Samantha. At this rate, Sarah was never going to get to dance with Amy.

"So, how about that dance? For old times' sake?" Robin asked, holding out her hand.

Sarah sighed. Despite their past, she couldn't help feeling a little sorry for Robin. Although Sarah had once envied the ease that Robin's wealth seemed to bring, really there was not much to envy at all. "Just one," she said, allowing herself to be led to the dance area.

After they began dancing, Robin spoke. "So I've been thinking of getting a new girlfriend."

Sarah didn't reply, unsurprised that Robin intended to jettison Angelique.

"I always liked you best," Robin continued. "What do you say you come with me on that whale-watching trip?"

Sarah looked at her in surprise. "Robin, this dance is one thing, but I don't want to go whale-watching with you and I don't want to get back together."

"We could go shopping, too."

"Shopping? Did you not listen to anything I just said? I don't care about shopping."

"Then why are you with another wealthy woman like Amy Bergen? I didn't know who she was in that lifeguard outfit, but I do now."

"It isn't like that," Sarah said.

"No?" Robin asked.

"No," Sarah answered. "Money may have been how you reeled me in, but it's not that way with her." Robin was so annoying. Sarah could kick herself for agreeing to this dance. "I didn't even know her last name was Bergen until—" Sarah stopped. She didn't need to explain herself to Robin.

"Until what?" Robin asked. "Oh, I see. Until after you slept with her." She snickered.

Sarah stopped dancing, but Robin held on to her. "Okay, okay, my apologies. Maybe you're a new woman, immune to the lure of money."

Sarah took a breath and reluctantly resumed dancing. Hopefully, the song would end soon.

"But you're clearly one of few such women here tonight," Robin said with a pointed look through the crowd of dancers at Amy. Amy was dancing with yet another woman, another woman who was pawing her. "There are obviously plenty of women eager to get their hands in Ms. Bergen's pockets and in more ways than one."

"I've had enough of this dance." Sarah pulled away from Robin and her insinuations and escaped back to the table.

Amy's suit jacket was draped over a chair. Upon seeing it, Sarah sagged because it meant Amy had been back and Sarah hadn't been here to reconnect with her, thanks to the dance with Robin. Amy had probably been waylaid by another groupie or auction donor and had left to dance again. Sarah was so frustrated she wanted to cry.

She looked at the dance area, scanning it for Amy. Yes, the woman now dancing with her was probably one of the donors, judging from her very expensive-looking dress. However, Sarah couldn't be certain. She could be a parent of one of the junior lifeguards, she could be anyone. All Sarah knew was that Amy was dancing with yet another woman who wasn't her.

Sarah pulled Amy's suit jacket off the chair and snugged it around her for comfort while she waited for Amy to return. It smelled deliciously of her and she pulled it more tightly around herself.

One of the jacket pockets was kind of bulky. Sarah patted it. Something soft was in there. She reached in. Lacy red underwear! What the hell? Amy didn't wear underwear like that—whose were they? Angelique's? Red to go with that red tube dress? Jesus! Sarah flung them aside.

What the hell else was in that pocket? She reached in again. A napkin with a lipstick kiss and a phone number? Hey, wasn't that Samantha's number? Wanted to talk about the dealership, my ass! She tossed the napkin aside.

Sarah dug around more in the pocket. What the...? Another napkin with a phone number? And with a smiley face under the number, no less. Maybe it went with those lacy red underwear. Ugh, she didn't even want to think about those.

And what was in the other pocket? A few business cards. Oh—so one pocket for business, one pocket for pleasure. Nice. Real nice.

Sarah jerked out of Amy's suit jacket and flung it onto a chair just as Justin and Ron bounded over from the dance area. "Hey, now, what's the matter?" Justin asked, taking gentle hold of her shoulder and scanning her face while Ron also looked on with concern.

Sarah wiped at her eyes. "Can you drive me home?"

"Sure, sweetie," Justin said. "We'll drive you home. We can go right now."

CHAPTER SIXTEEN

The next morning, still hurt and fuming and not in the mood to answer Amy's phone calls, Sarah went out to the backyard to do some weeding. Yanking weeds from the flower bed along the fence, she threw them into her gardening bucket.

Amy claimed not to be into flings and not to be into lifeguard groupies, but there she had been, collecting underwear and phone numbers all evening long! Maybe she just wanted something brief and simple after all. Maybe she just wanted someone fun and carefree, not someone complicated and serious who taught math and corrected her on how to give her cat a pill and tried to help her in the middle of doing her job in a rescue.

Sarah shook her head at herself. She had even bothered Amy with a question about whether she wanted kids. Amy had been a good sport about the question that night, but she probably hadn't even been thinking that far ahead, probably didn't even want to settle down. Come to think of it, she still hadn't introduced Sarah to any of her family, even though they all lived in the area and even though she saw them frequently for brunch.

Summer would be over soon. Maybe their time together was ending with the end of this fling season. Maybe Amy would rather just choose someone new from the women fawning over her. There was certainly no shortage for her to choose from! Those women were unbelievable, trying to steal Amy right out from under her. If they knew about the rescue from the newspaper articles and TV shows, then they knew that Amy had a girlfriend. Did it not matter at all to any of them? Did it not matter to Amy?

Amy parked and hurried up to Sarah's house. Sarah still wasn't answering her phone and Amy was still desperate to explain about last night.

After Amy had found her suit jacket splayed on the seat of a chair and Angelique's underwear on the ground nearby, along with the napkins with phone numbers on them, she had a pretty good idea of why Sarah had suddenly disappeared from the Lifeguard Luau. She had searched the Luau for Sarah, thinking that maybe she had taken a walk over to the silent auction again or to the catering tent, but she hadn't found her. She had tried her cell phone, wanting to apologize and explain, but Sarah hadn't answered. She had tried a few more times, but she still hadn't answered.

Amy had then sent a text to her asking her to confirm at least that she had gotten home all right. She had gotten a terse response of "yes" to that. Justin and Ron must have driven her home, since they had suddenly disappeared as well.

Amy had debated whether to drive over last night, but it was clear that Sarah didn't want to talk to her just then, so she had driven back to her condo instead. She was here now, though, and she had to get Sarah to listen. She rang the doorbell. There was no answer, so she rang again. Still no answer.

Sarah's car was here, so Sarah was probably here too unless she was out riding her bike. She could be ignoring the doorbell, but maybe she was in the shower or in the backyard where she couldn't hear it. Amy walked over to the fence and stood on tiptoe to peer over. Sarah was kneeling at a flower bed and pulling weeds with a certain amount of vigor. Amy girded herself for trouble and called out a greeting to her.

Sarah looked over at her. "What are you doing here?"

It wasn't the greeting she had hoped for, but it could have been worse. Amy offered her a smile. "Looking for you. Can I come in?"

Sarah hesitated but then got up to unlatch the gate and let her in. She looked her up and down, seeming to notice her slacks and blouse. "On your way to family brunch?"

Amy nodded. "Yes, and I was hoping you would join me. I'm sorry our evening got cut short. How about we continue our date today with brunch?"

Sarah blinked. She opened her mouth as if to say something but stopped. Amy couldn't blame her for not knowing what to say. If the rest of her night had been like Amy's, she probably had had all kinds of thoughts running through her mind and had been making herself crazy with worry. Especially over the things she had found in Amy's jacket pockets. But since brunch was the first thing Sarah asked about this morning, it was clearly important to her, something that Amy hadn't fully realized. Maybe Amy should have extended an invitation to her sooner, despite her misgivings about subjecting her to her difficult family.

"Last night wasn't very fun for me," Sarah finally said. "At least, not much of it. The parts with you were fun, but they were few and far between."

"I didn't know last night would be like that. I'm really sorry."

"Tell me, was the night fun for you?"

"No, not at all! I mean, apart from getting to have dinner with you and our friends, of course."

"So, you didn't have a good time dancing with all of those women and collecting underwear and phone numbers?"

"No! And I wasn't collecting… I wanted to dance with you! I didn't want to dance with any of those women! And I certainly didn't want their underwear and phone numbers!"

"No? Then why were they in your pocket?"

Amy heaved a sigh and spread her arms in exasperation. "They put them in there while we were dancing, and short of taking them out and dropping them on an empty dinner plate, I didn't know how to get rid of them!"

Sarah gave a little snort. "That would have been a sight for the caterers."

"Yes." Amy risked a small smile. "On the other hand, Samantha or Angelique might actually have gotten a phone call that way, because I have no plans to ever call either of them."

"No?"

"No."

Sarah shook her head. "Samantha and Angelique and some of those other women were something else. Robin is, too. I'm sorry you had to meet her again."

"I was surprised to see you dancing with her," Amy ventured.

"Yeah," Sarah said with a sigh. "Me too. She asked me and I was stupid enough to think that she might be able to be pleasant for a few minutes while we danced and you were with Angelique. I felt a little sorry for her that her girlfriend was all over you like an octopus."

Amy grinned.

Sarah scowled. "What's that grin for?"

"You were concerned that Angelique was all over me, not me all over her. Your real concern wasn't that I was interested in Angelique."

Sarah tilted her head as she pondered what Amy had said. "You're right. I wasn't concerned that you were interested in her—I could tell that you weren't."

Amy nodded. "I wasn't. And I wasn't interested in Samantha, either, or anyone else."

Sarah took a breath. "The more I think about it, the more I realize it. It's just… Everyone had their hands all over you, and then Robin… Robin was saying things, putting thoughts in my head. It was all making me a little crazy. And then I put on your suit jacket and found that stuff in your pocket. I just had to get out of there." She shook her head. "I'm sorry. I shouldn't have left last night."

"I wish you hadn't. It hurt. But I do understand. And the way Robin eyed you wearing that dress that hugged your body like a dream was enough to make me a little crazy, too."

Sarah smiled. "Thanks." Then her expression changed to one of consternation as she apparently remembered something else. "Can you believe that Robin invited me to go on a whale-watching charter with her?"

Considering the hungry way Robin had eyed Sarah a time or two, Amy wasn't surprised by the notion. "I hope you turned her down."

"Of course I did."

"Good, because she didn't win the bidding on that whale-watching charter—I did." Amy grinned at her.

"What? You won it?"

"Uh-huh." Amy nodded proudly. "Want to come with me?"

"You bet I do!" Sarah said. She rushed to Amy and hugged her. She pulled back in the circle of her arms and looked at her. "I had wanted to take you on it—that's why I bid on it. But how did you know? I didn't see you go into the auction tent."

"It was one of the places I looked when I couldn't find you. I happened to see that you had bid on the charter. And then I saw that Robin had bid next. When I saw the amount, I suspected she raised it that much just to upset you. I figured you must have wanted to go on the charter or you wouldn't have bid on it, so I bid on it too."

"Oh, Amy. Thank you. Thank you because we get to go on it after all, and thank you for beating Robin at her little game."

"My pleasure. I'm sorry I wasn't there to check out the silent auction with you in the first place."

Sarah gave a shrug. "It's okay. You were chatting with your coworkers, and then I kind of forgot about viewing the rest of the items up for bid after encountering Robin and Angelique."

"Angelique," Amy repeated with a shudder. "I learned more about her during that dance last night than I wanted to, that's for sure. Do you know that she told me she had just had a 'vajacial'?"

Sarah frowned in confusion, looking as perplexed as Amy had felt when Angelique mentioned it. "Is that what I think it might be?" Sarah asked.

"If you're thinking vaginal facial, or in Angelique's case, a facial for her 'va-jay-jay,' then yes. Apparently, it involved a scrub and a mask after her Brazilian."

"Ouch," Sarah said with a grimace.

"That's what I thought, too. But according to Angelique, it was a pleasant spa day for her 'lady parts.'"

Sarah raised her eyebrows.

"Yeah," Amy said. "It was a lot for me to take in, too. Especially since the only 'lady parts' I'm interested in are yours."

Sarah laughed. "Likewise. But can we stop calling them 'lady parts' now?"

"Yes, please," Amy said, laughing also.

Sarah's expression became serious again.

"What is it?" Amy asked.

Sarah took a breath. "I want to ask you something else. You and I started out with a fling. You made an exception about flings for me, so why not make an exception for any of those other women?"

"Because things are different now," Amy answered, gazing at her.

"How?"

"Because I love you," Amy said. "I don't want anyone else."

Sarah looked at her with such happy tenderness that Amy thought her heart would melt. "I love you, too," Sarah said.

Amy pulled her close again, kissing her and then hugging her tightly. She felt she could stay this way forever. But she also wanted to take Sarah to meet her family. "So, would you like to come to brunch today?"

"I thought you'd never ask," Sarah said, smiling.

"Yeah, I'm sorry about that. And I can see that it's made you doubt me. It's not that I haven't wanted to take you to brunch, it's just that my family can be difficult."

"I know you've mentioned that, but I think I'll be okay. I need to change into something nicer, though." Sarah looked down at her outfit of dirty gardening clothes. "A shower would be a good idea, too. Do I have time?'

"Sure, there's plenty of time," Amy said.

"Plenty of time? Does that mean you can join me in my bedroom after my shower?"

"It does." Amy grinned.

CHAPTER SEVENTEEN

"Here we are," Amy said to Sarah as she pulled in to the driveway of her parents' home and parked. "Ready for brunch?"

"Yes, but are you sure we aren't late?" Sarah asked.

Amy reached for Sarah's hand, brought it to her lips, and planted a reassuring kiss on it. "No, we aren't late. This is about the usual time I get here." In Sarah's bedroom, time had started to slip away from them, but what they had been doing had been too enjoyable to cut short. Just the memory of Sarah's heat against hers was enough to make Amy's center give a throb, the sensation making her inhale a short breath.

Sarah cast a knowing glance at her, smiling and raising an eyebrow.

Amy chuckled and gave her a quick kiss. "Really, we aren't late. Now come on, I want to introduce you to my family." They got out and walked up to the front door.

Unlocking the door with her key, Amy let them in. "Everyone will be in the living room. It's this way." She led Sarah into the living room, putting her arm around her waist as they stepped into the room. But no one was there. Amy had thought it had seemed too quiet. Where was everyone? Her sister, at least, and probably her husband Fred, were around here somewhere, because their SUV was in the driveway. Amy turned to Sarah. "On second thought, maybe they're starting outside on the patio today. They sometimes do." Amy shook her head; brunch was already off to an awkward start—just what she had been hoping to avoid.

"The weather is certainly lovely enough for that today," Sarah said.

Good, Sarah seemed unbothered at having to search for everyone. "Yes, the weather is lovely," Amy said as she led Sarah toward the back of the house to the patio. At hearing the muted sounds of conversation through the glass patio doors, she breathed a sigh of relief. But the clearer the sounds became, the less they sounded like casual conversation and more like a serious discussion. She stopped, with Sarah stopping alongside her. They looked through the glass to see what was going on.

Aurora, their parents, and Fred were all gathered and talking animatedly as they sat around the patio table. There were frowns, smiles, and a lot of gesticulating.

"I can't tell whether whatever is going on out there is good or bad, can you?" Amy asked.

"No, but whatever it is, it looks serious." As they continued to watch, Sarah asked, "You don't think it's anything to do with us, do you?"

Amy turned to her. "What do you mean?"

"You know, your bringing a girlfriend over. I know you said your family is gay-friendly, but I also know that people who say they are gay-friendly sometimes change their minds when faced with an actual gay couple."

"No, my family doesn't have a problem there, so don't worry about that. They got over anything like that a long time ago. I don't know what they're discussing so intently today, but I know it's not that." Amy reached over and squeezed her hand reassuringly.

"Okay, good. I was just checking." Sarah squeezed back.

"What my family talks about most is the auto business, so it's probably something to do with that. I just hope it's not another disagreement about my job. I thought they were moving past that now, but maybe I was wrong." She paused. "Would you like to leave?"

"Leave?" Sarah turned to her. "Amy, it doesn't look that bad out there. And we don't even know what they're discussing. Maybe they're discussing sports or politics."

Amy took a breath. "You're right. Maybe I'm overreacting." Brunches had been more civil ever since the conciliatory phone calls with her family after the pier rescue. The articles and interviews that she had done with the media had helped her family understand her motivations and point of view. They were now more accepting of her job change and the fact that she was going to sell her dealership. That's why she thought it would be okay for Sarah to come to family brunch now.

"There's one way to find out," Sarah said. She gestured at the door handle.

Amy reached for the handle. "I'm game, if you are."

Sarah nodded, and Amy slid the open door.

Her family looked up at the sound.

"Hi, everyone," Amy said, putting a smile on her face and stepping outside with Sarah. "What's going on back here?"

"Hello!" Her family members smiled and stood. The greeting seemed upbeat enough and Amy relaxed somewhat, but she looked to her dad for an answer to her question because she wanted to know what she and Sarah were getting into.

He answered, "Oh, just ironing out the details of an idea Aurora has. Now, how about introducing us to this lovely young lady." He smiled kindly at Sarah.

Amy didn't like being brushed off, but lately everyone had been making more of an effort not to get so caught up only in dealership talk at brunch and she appreciated it. As long as her father and the rest of her family were being polite to Sarah, she would let the brush-off pass. "Everyone," Amy said, "I'd like to introduce you to Sarah Wagner, my girlfriend." She then introduced Sarah to each of her family members.

"We're happy to meet you, Sarah," her mother said. "We're having Bellinis today. Would you like one? Or I can pour you the peach juice without the Prosecco, like Amy prefers, or we also have water."

Sarah smiled. "Yes, I'll have a Bellini, please."

"I can get the drinks, Mom," Amy walked over to the drink cart to prepare the drinks and her family retook their seats, with Aurora offering Sarah a seat next to her and Fred.

Amy listened to the conversation while she fixed the drinks. Aurora complimented Sarah's dress and the two of them were soon talking about new clothing colors for the upcoming fall season. If Aurora and their parents had been discussing business details, they must have resolved them, because Aurora and everyone else seemed fine now. Amy returned, handing Sarah the drink and taking a seat next to her with her own drink.

"Thank you," Sarah said. She took a sip. "This is good."

Amy's family nodded as they sipped their own drinks. Conversation resumed, with Sarah remarking on the loveliness of her parents' Craftsman-style furnishings and her parents telling the stories behind some of them.

When Emilia came out to announce that brunch was ready, everyone stood up, preparing to make their way back inside the house. Amy was a little disappointed for the conversation to end. If she'd known her family would be this pleasant, she would have brought Sarah here sooner. Drinks in hand, everyone began walking toward the door. Everyone except Aurora, who was hanging back and beckoning to their father.

"Dad," Aurora said, "one more thing…"

Ugh, Amy all but groaned. Just when things were going so smoothly and they were all about to sit down at the table together. She knew this pleasant brunch was too good to be true. If her sister and dad were going to pick up where they left off with their conversation, she hoped it wasn't going to result in an argument. She took a breath. As Sarah had pointed out earlier, maybe it would be okay. She walked into the house with the others, while Aurora and their father stayed outside. As her mother and Fred headed to the dining room, Amy took a moment to introduce Sarah to Emilia. Afterward, she led Sarah into the dining room

Only her mother and Fred were seated at the table, so apparently Aurora and her father were still talking. She wished they would finish soon or their delay would become rude. She pulled out a chair to seat Sarah and then took her own seat next to her. A moment later, her father and Aurora walked in and seated themselves as well. They seemed calm, so the topic of their conversation must not have been a problem. Amy wasn't going to ask about it again, though, and get another brush-off.

Before she had time to dwell on the situation any further, Emilia reappeared and served the meal. Brunch was bacon and cheese quiche today, the slices accompanied by a little tangle of baby greens in vinaigrette. Amy loved the flaky, buttery crusts on the quiches that Emilia prepared, and her mouth started watering. As always at brunch, the food would be good. She turned and smiled at Sarah, who smiled back at her.

Her father cleared his throat. "Before we eat, there is something we want to say."

Amy looked at him. This statement wasn't his usual way of beginning a toast at brunch and she felt her stomach sink, worried that this brunch was about to turn into something like the ones before the pier rescue. If it did devolve into an argument, she wouldn't let her family drag Sarah into it; she and Sarah would leave.

"Or, I should say," her father continued with a chuckle as he corrected himself, "Aurora is the one with something to say." He looked to Aurora, smiling.

Chuckling and smiling? Amy blinked and then looked across the table at Aurora.

"Amy," Aurora said, "I'd like to buy your dealership."

"God," Amy blurted, "is this what everyone's been discussing on the patio? I thought something was the matter!" She leaned back in her chair in relief. "We both did when we got here and saw you out there talking like that," she said with a glance at Sarah, reaching for her hand and giving it a squeeze.

"Oh, no, not at all!" Aurora exclaimed. "I just wanted to save the good news for the toast!"

"And we wanted to spend time today meeting Sarah," her mother said, sending a friendly smile to Sarah before turning back to Amy. "It isn't every day you bring a girlfriend to brunch, you know."

"I should hope not," Sarah interjected, and everyone laughed.

"Yes, the business discussion could wait today," her father said. "Because we enjoyed meeting Sarah and because I figured you could worry about selling your dealership just a little bit longer. After all, I have been." He winked at her.

Amy shook her head but smiled.

"So what do you think?" Aurora asked.

Amy turned to Aurora. "I'd love it if you were the one to buy my dealership. I'd much rather do business with you than with some of the people I've been talking to. But are you sure about it?" Amy needed her to be sure, because she was running out of time to sell and needed to know that Aurora wouldn't change her mind and the deal fall through.

"Yes, I'm sure. I'd been thinking of expanding and this will be a great way to do it." She paused and smiled. "And I'm pre-approved for a loan."

Amy smiled back. "I think I'm going to like doing business with you." She raised her glass, waiting for Aurora to do the same, and then touched her glass to hers. Everyone joined in the toast. Sarah leaned over to give her a kiss on the cheek and it gladdened Amy that she was here to share in this good news with her.

"I imagine everything will be settled by just about the time the junior lifeguard pier jump rolls around," her dad said.

She turned to him. "You remember the pier jump?"

"Of course we remember," her mother answered. "You were always one of the first ones off the pier. Scared us half to death each time, even though you always did the jump so well."

Her dad nodded. "The kids doing the jump this year are lucky that you will be the one to teach them how it's done."

Amy smiled.

CHAPTER EIGHTEEN

Sarah and Justin wound their way through the maze of beach chairs and beach towels of the crowd gathered on South Coast Beach, searching for an open space from which to watch the junior lifeguards participate in the rite of passage that was the South Coast Beach pier jump.

"How about over there?" Sarah asked as she spied a patch of sand that still looked spacious enough to accommodate two more beach towels.

"Good eye," Justin said, hastening to the empty spot with her.

Unfurling their towels, they took a seat and joined the rest of the spectators in looking toward the pier. The tall pier was lined with junior lifeguards in their signature red swim trunks or red swimsuits. Amy was up there, too, and with the other instructors, would be supervising the jumps into the water below.

Sarah knew how thrilled Amy was to be managing her first junior lifeguard pier jump, and Sarah was thrilled for her. Amy had worked hard for her space up there as an instructor and Sarah couldn't imagine her as anything else. Especially not as a general manager at an auto dealership. Thank goodness the worry about that was over, now that the sale of the dealership to Aurora was finalized. Going on the whale-watching private charter with Amy this evening was going to be a fun way to both celebrate and relax.

"It's going to be kind of scary to watch the kids jump from something that high," Justin said with a shudder.

"Yes, it really is high. Amy's mom told me she was barely able to keep from covering her eyes when Amy did the jumps as a kid."

"And yet, some of these people around us were crazy enough to bring binoculars for a closer look." He shook his head as if in disbelief.

"I wish I had a pair of binoculars, because I know just who I'd zoom in on up there."

"Who? Peter?" Justin asked with a teasing grin.

"No," Sarah said as she swatted at him. "Amy, of course." Just the thought of Amy's toned body tantalizingly revealed in that red swimsuit of hers was enough to drive Sarah to distraction.

"Oh, hey, I think they're starting." Justin pointed up at the pier, where two lifeguards were unlatching and removing a section of the pier railing. From this distant vantage point on the beach, it was hard to identify the individual lifeguards on the pier, but Sarah recognized Amy's movements and watched as she and the other lifeguard motioned to one of the junior lifeguards to step forward.

The crowd murmured excitedly.

"I would be so terrified," Justin said.

"Me too," Sarah said. But if the young girl who stepped forward was afraid, it didn't show.

Amy guided the girl through the opening and around to the remaining section of railing, where the girl positioned herself so that she faced out over the ocean with her hands grasping the railing behind her, just as Amy had the night she had leapt from the pier. Amy bent toward the girl to speak, and Sarah imagined that she was giving her some last words of advice and encouragement.

After barely a moment's pause, the girl jumped out and away from the pier. Sarah, Justin, and the rest of crowd gave a collective gasp of awe. In the air, the girl brought her arms down by her sides, keeping her legs together and slightly bent as she entered the water with a splash. She resurfaced quickly and Sarah and Justin cheered loudly along with the rest of the crowd.

The jumps continued, with each jumper waiting for the previous one to swim safely from the area. Hannah, Mandy, and some of her other students and some of Justin's students were among those who would be jumping, and Sarah was proud of all of them. Some kids took a few moments longer than others before making the decision to jump, which Sarah found completely understandable, but most jumped without hesitation. They were all impressive kids, and Sarah hoped that some of them would grow up to be talented lifeguards like Amy.

Justin turned to her with a smile. "Looks like your lifeguard taught these kids well," he said, clearly thinking similar thoughts about the poise and skill of the junior lifeguards during this feat.

"Yes," Sarah said. And this time, she felt no uncertainty in response to Justin's use of the phrase "your lifeguard," because after her summer together with Amy, Amy did feel like hers now. And Sarah was really looking forward to their date after the pier jump was complete.

CHAPTER NINETEEN

"Do you think we'll see some whales?" Sarah asked Amy as they walked down the dock in the late afternoon light toward the small yacht that was to be their private charter for their whale-watching excursion.

Amy chuckled. "I think I might have heard a question a lot like that on the drive here." She put her arm around Sarah and pressed a kiss to her temple.

"Yeah, you might have," Sarah admitted. She knew she was overly excited about the cruise.

"The cruise is two hours long, so I think we'll have a good chance of seeing something," Amy said.

They reached the yacht, a sleek white boat that had plenty of windows and that looked like it would give a smooth, comfortable ride on the ocean.

"Welcome aboard," said a bearded, gray-haired man who introduced himself as the captain and then introduced his crew members. One was a woman named Nancy who was a marine naturalist. From the extra-welcoming smile she gave them,

Sarah had the impression she was family, which made her feel immediately comfortable aboard the yacht.

Before they left the dock, the captain gave them a brief overview of the boat or "vessel" as he called it. The interior of the boat reminded Sarah of that of an upscale motorhome she had once seen on TV, with high quality and cleverly arranged cabinetry and seating, all of which was firmly fastened in place. She and Amy settled into comfy, built-in, sofa-style seats at a table.

As the boat got underway, Nancy took a seat near them, telling them about the whales and other marine life they might see. Sarah exchanged excited glances with Amy, even more hopeful that they would see something. After Nancy finished her chat, she excused herself and left the table.

"Would you care for some refreshments?" The other crew member brought a cheese and cracker plate and then returned with two wine glasses and poured them each a glass of cabernet sauvignon.

Sarah took in the thoughtfully provided drinks and snacks on the table, the panoramic view of the sparkling ocean and sunny coastline through the windows, and the woman she loved beside her. "I already love this cruise no matter what we'll see."

"I'll drink to that. I love being here with you." Amy touched her glass to Sarah's, and they sipped their wine.

"Would you like to go out on the rear deck if it's not too cold?" Amy asked.

"Yes, it would be fun to feel the breeze for a little while," Sarah said. She had worn a jacket for the boat ride. Amy had worn a thick, navy blue, quarter zip pullover sweater with a stand collar that looked nice and warm. Not to mention sexy. It brought out her agate-colored eyes and made Sarah want to run her hands through her short, sable brown hair and then kiss her senseless. But she could wait to do that, for a little while at least.

They carried their wine outside and took a seat on one of the two small, cushioned seating areas. The breeze was invigorating but not uncomfortable. Amy put her arm around her and Sarah leaned close. The boat must have reached the desired distance from shore, because it was now cruising parallel to the coast. Sipping their wine, they watched the vast sea and endless shoreline.

Amy turned to Sarah and sighed a happy sigh. "I haven't felt so relaxed and carefree in a long time. I've been so anxious about finding a buyer for my dealership in time to let me keep my job as a lifeguard that I have been worrying for months. But now that the sale is taking place, I don't have to worry about any of those things any longer."

Sarah laid her hand on Amy's back and caressed her to comfort her. "I imagine it feels like a weight has been lifted from you."

"It does," Amy said. "I thought I might not even get to be there with the junior lifeguards during the pier jump. And I worried that this whale-watching excursion with you might be our last bit of fun this summer before I had to give up being a lifeguard and go back to work at my dealership. Worst of all, I was worried that I would become so unhappy having to go back to my dealership job that my discontent would scare you away like it has other girlfriends."

"If things hadn't gone the way you wanted, I'd like to believe that I wouldn't have been scared away. I love you too much."

"I love you very much, too." Amy squeezed her hand and looked at her tenderly. "You've been by my side during so much of this tough time. I know all of it's been a stressful experience for you, too, even with it working out. But you believed in me and you stayed."

Sarah smiled at her. Things had been stressful, but their relationship was stronger for it. She sipped her wine and then stared contemplatively at it. "You know," she said, "my friend Justin has a habit of comparing wine and relationships."

"Oh?" Amy asked.

"Yes." Sarah held up her glass of cabernet sauvignon. "For example, he thinks the cabernet sauvignon of relationships is serious and robust. I'd like to think that our relationship is like that." She smiled at Amy.

"Hmm, I like the sound of that," Amy said. "You know what I've heard about a red wine like cabernet sauvignon too?"

"What?" Sarah asked.

"That it's good for longevity," Amy said with a smile. "I'd also like to think our relationship will have that."

Sarah touched her glass to Amy's. "To longevity." She took a sip.

Amy took a sip of her wine also. Then, setting her glass down and collecting Sarah's glass to set it down as well, she reached for her, gently cupped her face in her hands, and kissed her.

Sarah savored the kiss and the depth of emotion behind it; the kiss felt like a promise. She was so caught up in it that it took her a moment to register the sound of a large splash some distance from the boat. Amy broke the kiss, clearly registering the sound as well. "Look!" Sarah cried, jumping to her feet and pointing. A whale was rolling playfully in the water, one of its huge flippers sending up a spray of water every now and again.

"Oh, wow!" Amy stood, too.

"And there's another one! See that giant puff of mist?"

"Yeah! That must be from its spout." Amy turned to Sarah. "I have my phone with me. Do you want to take some pictures of them?"

"No, that's okay. I'll remember all of this with you."

"I will too." Amy smiled.

Yes, Sarah would remember everything about this summer. And as she gazed at Amy and thought of all the summers and years they would share together, summer felt infinite.

Bella Books, Inc.

Women. Books. Even Better Together.

P.O. Box 10543
Tallahassee, FL 32302

Phone: 800-729-4992
www.bellabooks.com